…rt Story
Award 2019

with Cambridge University

First published in Great Britain in 2019 by Comma Press.
www.commapress.co.uk

A CIP catalogue record of this book is available
from the British Library.

ISBN 1-912697-22-X
ISBN-13 978-1-91269-722-9

The publisher gratefully acknowledges the support
of Arts Council England.

Printed and bound in Great Britain by Clays Ltd, Elcograf S.p.A

BBC NATIONAL SHORT STORY AWARD 2019

Contents

Introduction

THE WORLD IS DIVIDED into two kinds of people; those who recognise that a perfect short story is the greatest literary achievement, and those who we need to convert to this way of thinking!

I have loved the form for as long as I've been a reader, and have valued and heralded the authors who have moved, impressed and beguiled me over the years. There are too many to list, but Carson McCullers, Jhumpa Lahiri, Roald Dahl and Kazuo Ishiguro are particular favourites of mine.

Short stories are not a warm up for the 'real thing' as some would have us believe. They are gifts of concision, they demand one's total attention, and I relish devouring, digesting, being moved and surprised by a perfectly-formed short work. It has, therefore, been a privilege to judge this year's BBC National Short Story Award with Cambridge University, and to take the role of chair.

Unlike my fellow judges, I didn't go to university so I don't have the academic qualifications (apart from A-Level English!) that you might mistakenly imagine are all-important for this role. However, what I hope I've brought to proceedings is my internationalist view of the world, and a deep-rooted passion for making the arts accessible.

As a broadcaster whose expertise lies in arts and culture, I've travelled the globe extensively and I've met, interviewed and spent time with some of the most extraordinary creative minds imaginable: writers, directors, visual artists, actors, musicians and dancers. What they all have in common is that they seek to move us, to make us think, to transform us, and I strongly believe all five of the shortlisted writers and stories gathered here do all that and more.

They are rich and gorgeous works on paper, and I'm so delighted that they'll all be given an actual voice when they're recorded and broadcast on BBC Radio 4. As a reader, one can imagine and create the sounds and rhythms of a character in one's head, but hearing a story as the author intended is always quite magical. This year, we have some very distinctive and memorable voices in the mix; stories that have very different strengths and kinds of appeal.

I need to be honest with you, choosing these five stories was not an easy process. When I say this year's shortlist was a hard-fought contest, I'm putting it mildly. The judging was so close at one point that we implemented the Prix Goncourt voting system, and even that didn't help! We agonised over our decisions and disagreed vociferously at times, but on the whole, the debating and fighting was carried out in a civilised manner. By most of us anyway. Fortunately, my fellow judges and I each brought something different to the table and we appreciated each other's highly considered opinions.

Author Richard Beard was polite, brilliant and forceful in his statements, and he deeply understands the human condition. He's written six novels, four books of narrative non-fiction and he won the 2018 PEN/Ackerley prize for his memoir *The Day That Went Missing*.

The preternaturally gifted writer Daisy Johnson was a highly articulate judge, and the piece she wrote for *The Guardian* about reasons to love short stories could very well be a future manifesto for this award. In 2018, she became the youngest ever author to be shortlisted for The Man Booker Prize for her first novel *Everything Under,* and her short story collection *Fen* won the 2017 Edge Hill Short Story Prize.

Author Cynan Jones brought forth strong emotional responses to some of the stories in contention, as well as his great knowledge and appreciation for the form. It was a given that our finalists would be able to combine the five elements that make a great short story: character, setting, conflict, plot and theme, but Cynan made us all consider certain stories on a different level. He's written five novels and he won this very award in 2017.

And finally, the book-mother to us all, Di Speirs. As the Books Editor for BBC Radio she's an advocate of the formidable power of the short story, and as the regular judge on the panel, she naturally brought her expertise to bear. Di takes the 'iron fist in a velvet glove' approach to debate.

The five stories we've chosen transported us to new places; physically, emotionally, mythologically and culturally.

'Ghillie's Mum' by Lynda Clark tells the beautiful but painful story of a boy whose mother is a shapeshifter. She turns herself into animals and, as Ghillie reaches adolescence, he realises that he too has the gift. It's a moving, contemporary tale about being othered and made to feel different.

Jo Lloyd's 'The Invisible' is set in Wales in a time past, but also takes us to an otherworldly place through Martha, who is the only person who can see the 'Invisible'. It is enchanting, and there's a fabulist element to the story with readers being introduced to the Tylwyth Teg and Twrch Trwyth.

'Silver Fish in the Midnight Sea' by Jacqueline Crooks also has an otherworldly element. Sound-Ghost and the malevolent duppy are seen through the eyes of children who create their own world all day in the garden whilst their mother, recovering from her nightshifts, drifts back to her Caribbean island as she sleeps. The family are Jamaican with a mixed African and Indian heritage, and the story is told in delicious patois.

'It is unbearable, the thought that a child will not remember its mother.' Motherhood is at the centre of Lucy Caldwell's story 'The Children'. An effective paralleling of two young women's lives in different times, both fearing, but for very different reasons, that their children would be motherless. Their stories are also threaded through with current descriptions of asylum seekers in America having their children taken away from them at the border.

And finally, 'My Beautiful Millennial' by Tamsin Grey takes us through a young woman's decision to stop infantilising and demeaning herself for her boring, older lover who lives at the end of the Metropolitan Line in Amersham, and to take back her agency. The melancholy weight of the suburbs and a mangled pigeon help the process.

Intrigued?

Read on…

Nikki Bedi, London, 2019

The Children

Lucy Caldwell

TRUMPINGTON STREET IS SCULPTURAL in the sunshine: slashes and rhomboids of light and stark shade. Traffic is heavy and the taxi travels slowly, the driver giving me the tour. The Fitzwilliam, the Pitt Building, Peterhouse. We've already had The Backs, the Mathematical Bridge, designed by Isaac Newton and made, the taxi driver says, without a single nut or bolt. Students took it apart once to see how it worked and were unable to put it back together. I know this isn't true. Newton died a quarter of a century before the bridge was built, and it does have bolts, iron spikes driven in at angles obscured from sight. I walked over this bridge almost every day for the best – or worst – part of three years. But somehow the moment to say this passed, and so I smile and nod and let my mind drift.

I'm writing a story about Caroline Norton, who *changed the lot of mothers forever* with her battle to reform child custody law, or so the blurb on her biography says. I have the biography in a tote bag, though that's as much as I've read of it so far, along with a sheaf of her poems, newly-joined now by a raft of photocopies about marriage and Victorian law and women's quests for equality. I've just come from Girton College, the first women's college in Cambridge; dusty sunlight in high-ceilinged, book-lined rooms, parquet-floored corridors and a lunch buffet (poached salmon, potatoes, mixed sweetcorn and peas) under the patient lights of a hotplate in the Fellows' Dining Room. A communal jug of tapwater, tasting faintly of pewter. Polite tones in respectable surroundings; it all sounds eminently reasonable; Caroline Norton's letters to the Rt. Hon.s, her pamphlets, her famous essay condemning child labour; her Bills presented to the House of Lords. I'll read the texts, write the piece.

The ghost of my former self, indulged all this June day long, weaving on a rusty bike to and from the Sidgwick Site and the UL with a backpack of books, sitting earnestly on threadbare sagging armchairs, is lost to a sudden battery of car horns from behind and an outburst from the driver, who's pulled up abruptly somewhere he shouldn't. We're here. My husband and children are waiting for me in the Botanic Gardens. I pay him and sling the tote over my shoulder and go, all else forgotten.

The following day, I find a lump in my breast.

It's not unduly concerning at first. I'm breastfeeding; it's probably nothing; it will probably go. It doesn't go. A week passes, then another. It is larger now, and definitely there. I Google: breast lumps when to be concerned. Google suggests, as Google always does, that it could be terminal and it could be nothing. I phone the GP surgery, who – uncharacteristically – say they can see me tomorrow, name a time. Ok, great, I say, not sure if I feel reassured or more worried.

The next morning, dodging the breakfast scramble, I grab the untouched tote. The surgery is busy and always running late: it will be a good chunk of reading time. In the waiting room, blocking out the TV giving diabetes advice on a loop, the crying pre-schoolers at the vaccination clinic, the elderly man with a hacking cough, the mother chastising her bored, fighting sons in Bengali, I take out the biography. *Cut off from her children after an acrimonious split, she went about changing the law for wives and mothers.*

Right, I say to the portrait on the cover, a languorous oil painting in an off-the-shoulder dress, gold and ruby bracelets and elaborate lacquered hair, delicately holding a quill. Here we go.

★

I skim through Caroline's parents and her early years until – as she puts it – she accepts a proposal of marriage so that her life can begin.

There's a whole story in the titles of Caroline's songs, the first things she ever wrote. From before her marriage: 'Rosalie my Love, Awake!' 'Dry Up that Sparkling Tear,' 'The Home Where my Childhood Played,' 'Never Forget Me Love.' Afterwards: 'Oh Sad, Sad is the Heart,' 'Why Should I Sing of Days Gone By?' and 'Love Not.' The Honourable – or not so – George Chapple Norton mocks her letters and her ambitions, sets her writing things ablaze. He buys himself a cabriolet with her royalties – the word comes from the French, meaning *caper*, because of its light, bounding motion – a fancy and entirely unpractical vehicle. But when the doctor tells her to get some sea air to relieve the nausea of her second pregnancy, she is forced to share a bed with the landlady to save money. He slaps her face, he beats her. He seizes her by the nape of the neck and dashes her down on the floor. He kicks her in the side so hard that she can't sit down for days. He pulverises her face so badly the sight of it makes her sister vomit. He orders her from 'his' seat at the breakfast table and when she refuses, he takes the boiling tea-kettle and presses it down on her hand. Then he sits in her place and calmly eats his breakfast. She leaves him. He begs her to take him back. She takes pity on him and, for the sake of their boys, gives him another chance. Within two days, he beats her so badly she loses her unborn child. He leaves her bleeding on the floor and goes to shoot grouse in Scotland, refusing to pay the doctor's bill, leaving her to beg her brother for money. For weeks afterwards, she sits looking at raindrops on the window: *I begin to think I must have lost my soul.*

My name is called. But the GP wants a second opinion and asks me to return to the waiting room until her colleague is free. There are no chairs now so I stand against the wall. A weeks-old baby wails in pain and my body responds with the swell and rush of milk. I text my husband, who's meant to be back at work by now, instructions on what to feed the baby for lunch. I fish the book from my tote bag again, then hesitate. A moment:

what we used to call *a goose walking over my grave*.
This isn't how it was supposed to go. A second
opinion. I was expecting, Oh, it's just a milk duct,
use hot compresses and a comb. I was even
prepared for, Let's aspirate it now, a dab of local
anaesthetic and it'll only take a minute. It's
suddenly not what I want to read about anymore;
mothers, children, loss. I text my husband again.
It's all fine here, he texts me back, with a row of
Xs. Of course it is. He's a brilliant father. We're
equal partners. But still.

Don't be silly, I tell myself, and force my hands
to stop trembling and open the book.

Her brother tells her to come to his house in
Dorset for Easter, with the children, without
George. Her husband forbids it. She doesn't know
what to do. She decides to wait until he's at work,
and then sneak away. But he makes his move first.
She returns home one morning to find the
children, and their nanny, gone.

Frantic, she manages to bribe it out of a
footman that they've been taken to a lodging
house in Upper Berkeley Street, ahead of plans
to spirit them up North. She rushes to the house
and begs the servants there to let her see her
children, just for an hour, just for five minutes,
just to tell them she loves them. But their

master's instructions are clear and his threats severe, and they refuse.

I could hear their little feet running over my head while I sat sobbing below, only the ceiling between us and I not able to get to them!

Her eldest is recovering from scarlet fever. She doesn't trust her husband with their second, whom he taunts and dislikes, and the youngest is still a baby. She is desperate. But there's nothing she can do. The children are George's property, his to do with or dispose of as he sees fit, until they reach their majority at twenty-one. He sends them to his sister in Scotland. He changes the youngest child's name. When the middle child needs to be 'corrected', he is stripped naked, tied to a bedpost and whipped with a riding crop. She sees them one day in London for a few, snatched minutes. They are nervous wrecks, the middle one *a perfect skeleton*. They do not understand why she has abandoned them. They beg her to stay. Her heart aches with the weight of all that is impossible to explain. The following day, a message from her husband: the boys will not be seeing her again.

The years pass.

The second GP frowns and says carefully that although it is probably nothing, it is certainly something, and she'll refer me to the Breast Clinic at St Bart's. She taps away at her computer. I'll get a phone call in a few days to arrange the appointment. Out in the street, I finish the last few pages of the chapter I'm on. George writes to 'my Carry' that the boys are so grown-up that she would not recognise them if she passed them in the street. He offers to send her portraits he's commissioned. He says she can see them again if she comes back and submits herself to him. He forges letters from her, including one to the children saying their father wants them to die so he'll have fewer of them to keep. He says she can have them back if she engages a female companion of his choice. When she agrees, he immediately backtracks. He tells her she can see them at Christmas. He writes that they have embarked on the steamer SS Dundee. The day after they should have arrived, he tells her they have not come after all. He says they can join her on holiday. She rents a house by the sea, lights fires, airs the rooms. Ten days after they are supposed to be there, they still have not come. George says she can see them in London instead. She abandons the house and returns to London. He says he's changed his mind.

You have made, she writes to him, *an orphanage of our lives.*

I text my husband to tell him I'm on my way home. All ok, I ask, with you and the children? All fine, he texts back. Ok with you? And my fingers, fumbling, don't know what to say.

★

There is a famous house on Folgate Street in Spitalfields, about fifteen minutes' walk from me (or twenty if pushing a buggy one-handed and trailing a child on a scooter). It belonged to a man named Denis Severs, and he left it as a museum of sorts – part-museum, part-art installation – with the intention that as you walk through the doors, you feel that you are stepping through the surface of a painting. The house's ten rooms are ten 'spells', from the cellar and the piano nobile to the Smoking Room and the boudoir, transporting you back to the Huguenot silk-weavers who first lived there in the early eighteenth century, and on through the Victorian era, following the family's – and society's – fortunes. The porcelain, the portraits, the clink of the old brass clock: it feels as if the house's real inhabitants have just momentarily left the room that you've stepped into. Or so the website says. You cannot wear stiletto heels or heavily-ridged soles on your visit; it goes without saying that you cannot bring a buggy, or a boisterous child. They have night-time openings, which are called Silent Nights, where you leave your phone at the door, and general admission on Sundays and Mondays. My husband leaves work at lunchtime to come and look after the children in a nearby park so I can see the house. But somehow I've misread the website. It's a Wednesday: the house is closed.

They were not like us, the historian at Girton College said. We often think of the Victorians as basically the same as us; a bit stricter, more sentimental, maybe, but they were not like us at all. Imagine that almost everything we believe, all that we take for granted, is overturned. That's how far we are from them, that distance and then some again.

They tell you to allow a whole half-day for the clinic. There are ultrasounds, mammograms, radiographers, registrars to see; pieces of pink and white paper to be taken to different reception desks on different floors, filed in different buff-coloured folders. I find a corner seat, then move when I realise it's by a rack of leaflets with titles such as: *Cancer and Pregnancy*, and *Preparing a Child for Loss*. The clinic is also the oncology centre and there are women here at every stage of treatment, from potential diagnoses to full-blown weekly chemo. There are women in wheelchairs, bloated with steroids. A woman my age takes the seat beside me and smiles brightly, about to start up conversation. She is wearing a hospital gown and has a cannula taped to the back of her left hand. I look away and make random marks in the margins of my sheaf of papers until I sense her resolve, or solidarity, waning.

In the various waiting rooms, I pore over Caroline's letters in digitised archives online, as she takes her personal loss and transmutes it into something greater than her; something heroic, enduring, revolutionary. Her handwriting elegant and legible even on the screen of a phone, the curve of her uppercase *I* and curlicue on uppercase *C;* the cups of *y*s and *g*s that are dropped when she's writing with haste.

She dreams her husband is dying, attended by two old women who berate her. She dreams an unborn baby has drowned: *I saw him float away and no one would attend to me because I was mad!* Since they were born, I've dreamed of losing my babies, too. I dream that I've left my daughter in a Left Luggage unit and there are hundreds of dully-gleaming lockers and I don't have a key. I get off a long-haul flight and my phone starts ringing: my husband, thousands of miles away, is asking where on earth I am and in the background the baby's crying, desperate for me, and it's too late to undo what I've done. I am dying, and I'm scared, and they tell me to keep calm and hold the hands that reach down for me, and I do, and feel myself pulled from my body. A moment's relief, then the agony of realising I will never hold my children again. I beg for one last chance and am let sink back into my body, sore and clumsy, and I take my boy into my lap and hold him tight, the smooth, warm curve of his back, and know that this is all that matters, ever, ever, ever.

Caroline, without her boys – her Penny, her abandoned chicken Brin, her Too-Too the little tadpole – stays awake all night long, night after night, staring into the dark until visions of their large brown eyes swim up, *as when I looked up from my work and found them watching.*

She would be annoyed with them, then, for interrupting her; for breaking the spell. She writes – has always written – to survive. Her first novel paid for the birth of her son; the doctor's bills and the nurses. She accedes to her publisher's demand and writes a *Bijou Almanac* designed for the Christmas market; an inch and a half wide and sold with its own miniature eyeglass. She tries her hand at plays; she'll turn her pen to anything. She always has and has always had to, children or no.

She tests out guilt and refuses to feel guilty. Refuses shame, too: there is too much fear of publishing about women, she writes. It is reckoned that they wish nothing better than to hide themselves away and say no more about it. *No longer!* She writes. She will tell her truth, and she will change the world.

When I can't concentrate on Caroline's letters any longer, I read Twitter instead, swiping, tapping, swiping. In the US, the children of asylum seekers are being taken from their parents at the border. There are photographs on social media of minibuses fitted with rows of baby-carriers for transporting infants to 'tender age' shelters. There is shaky hand-held footage and anonymous testimony. Children led away from their parents to be bathed, never to come back. Breastfeeding babies pulled from their mother's arms. Sobbing toddlers clinging. A newsreader breaks down on live TV, unable to read the autocue. The US President rants on Twitter, self-righteous, or affecting outrage. I think of George Norton, suspicious, capricious, belligerent, ploddingly unintelligent, an ungovernable child. *Foaming and stamping and rambling from one accusation to another, so that it was impossible to make out,* wrote a clergyman attempting to mediate, *what he wanted, or whom he meant to attack.*

Laura Barrera, an attorney at the UNLV Immigration Clinic in Las Vegas, Nevada, tweeting from Paradise, NV.

> @abogada_laura | 5.55PM Jun 28, 2018
>
> My 5-yr-old client can't tell me what country she is from. We prepare her case by drawing pictures with crayons of the gang members that would wait outside her school. Sometimes she wants to draw ice cream cones and hearts instead. She is in deportation proceedings alone.

I read and read the stories online, unable to look away. A six-year-old who is blind, and her nonverbal four-year-old brother; nonverbal, in part, because he's traumatised. An attorney quoted on the BBC: 'Even a five-year-old who wasn't traumatised can't always tell you their address or what their parents look like or their last names. How do you expect a child to do all that? This is not something that the kids or their parents will ever get over.'

They do the scans; in a darkened room they do a biopsy. The results will be back within seven to ten days; the receptionist makes an appointment for exactly two weeks' time for me to come back and speak with the specialist. Back home, I quiz my not-yet four-year-old son: what's your full name? What's mine and daddy's? What's our address? Half of the time, he gets most of it almost right.

★

July. The UK prepares for the US Presidential visit. On the morning of 13th July, I watch over livestream as protestors launch the huge inflatable baby, with its snarling, lopsided mouth and piss-in-the-snow-hole eyes, to float above the Palace of Westminster. My son and I have made our placards, sellotaping pieces of A4 card to sticks of bamboo, and we intend to join the protest march. But at the last minute, the stupefying heat of the day, the thought of the sweltering tube, my husband delayed on the other side of the city, we – I – chicken out. My son is relieved: worried that the man who steals children will try to take him. I will do this, he says, and bares his teeth in a chimp-like snarl. I will do that, and the bad man will run away. Then he buries himself in my side. I want to stay with you for all the days and all the nights.

Yes, I say. Yes.

Later, I look at the best placards on Twitter. Mary Poppins, carrying her iconic umbrella, beside a slogan in rainbow colours: SUPER CALLOUS FRAGILE RACIST FACIST NAZI POTUS. We will overcomb the hate. Orange is the New Nazi. I'm missing Wimbledon for this, you Tangerine WANKMAGGOT. Ours simply said, BREASTFEEDING BABIES BELONG WITH THEIR MAMAS, and, even more simply, NO KIDS IN CAGES.

Caroline to Lord Melbourne: I wish I had never had children – pain and agony for the first moments of their life – dread and anxiety for their uncertain future – and now all to be a blank.

In the evenings, after he's gone to bed, I arrange my son's collection of dinosaurs to look like they're building a tower with his sister's bricks, racing his double-decker bus and her push-along trolley. I think of The Fairies who lived in my dolls' house and occasionally left letters, tiny writing in cards no bigger than postage stamps, and packets of Parma Violets. But my sisters and I were older, then: he will barely remember any of this. Do you remember before your sister was born? I ask him, and he thinks about it and says, No! He thinks some more and says, I hurt my knee in Croatia, which is true, he did, a bad graze falling off a low wall, and the shock of the blood made him howl for an hour.

In good moments, Caroline is convinced that there is still hope. *Let them do all they can about the children,* she writes, *I will undo in two hours what they have laboured to do for ten years – I have a power beyond brute force to swing them round again, back to their old moorings.* But mostly she feels the lethargy of despair. *No future can ever wipe out the past, nor renew it.* The children won't recognise her if she passes them in the street, nor she them. The youngest is no longer the fair, fat baby he used to be: those months, those years, those precious days, are lost forever.

It is unbearable, the thought that a child will not remember its mother.

There is a psychoanalyst who says that at a certain moment in pregnancy, if the mother-to-be is pregnant with a baby girl, five generations fuse together. It comes at around twenty weeks' gestation, when the unborn child, in her tiny, seedling ovaries, makes the hundreds of tiny eggs which will be her future children, or the possibility of them. In that moment, the not-yet-child is already mother; the not-yet-mother already grandmother; just as the mother-to-be was once a possibility inside her own in utero mother, carried by her one-day grandmother. I like the Escher's staircase of it, the sense of nestled Russian dolls. The potential grandchildren that I might never even see joined in a vertiginous rush with the grandmother who only barely met me, the centuries collapsing.

But the psychoanalyst uses the image to explain how suffering is passed down the generations; how we become trapped in the behaviours of our parents and theirs, doomed to repeat destructive patterns unless we find ways of breaking free. The iniquities, as the Bible solemnly tolls, visited unto the third and the fourth generations. The loss of a mother may be played out in the souls of your children's grandchildren.

The lawyers at RAICES, Texas's largest immigration legal service non-profit, estimate that at least a quarter of the children, a number in the hundreds, will never, ever be reunited with their parents again.

I bought the psychoanalyst's book because someone quoted him on Twitter saying that the US President was doing exactly the job he needed to, forcing into consciousness some of our collective unconscious issues. He told us not to look at him, but to look to ourselves. I didn't know quite what I made of this. The notion that we get the people we deserve, or require, seemed to let an individual off the hook; or conversely, to imply that their achievement wasn't that great. I think of Caroline, and Abogada Laura. At night, the children tumble through my dreams. I wake in a tangled sweat. I can't even go to a fucking march. In her cot beside me, the baby whimpers. I sit for hours, years, until my breathing calms.

She changes the law, single-handedly, but it's too late for her. The elder boys at 10 and 8 are beyond the law's reach; the youngest, so long as his father keeps him in Scotland, is beyond its jurisdiction, too. Little William Norton dies of lockjaw – tetanus – one Monday in September, aged just 9, after falling from his horse and cutting his arm. The boys are alone and unsupervised at their uncle's house, the only servant is the gamekeeper's wife, a hunched old woman who opens gates and locks doors. Willie makes his way to the nearest neighbour, Chapel Thorpe Hall, where he collapses and is put to bed. By the time Caroline's told that he's unwell, he has already died. She learns that he was conscious when he died, and begged for her, again and again.

The doctor tells Caroline that young Willie bore the painful spasms *with a degree of courage which he has rarely seen in so young a child*, as if this offers any consolation.

★

I am tired. I try to make my mind let go. This moment, and this, and this. Here, now; my baby's silky hair and milky smell. *A-duh*, she says, when she wakes in the night and wants milk. Online, a mother was alerted to breast cancer when her six-month old started refusing to nurse from one side. Online, another, still nursing twins, died ten days after her diagnosis. It is the night before the biopsy results. Somewhere in windowless rooms, cells have been scraped and splayed on slides, dyed and magnified and studied, pronounced upon. I have finished the biography, and the letters, and now I read the poems until I know sections of them by heart.

> *If the lulled heaving ocean could disclose*
> *All that has passed upon her golden sand,*
> *When the moon-lighted waves triumphant rose,*
> *And dashed their spray upon the echoing*
>   *strand:*
> *If dews could tell how many tears have mixed*
> *With the bright gem-like drops that Nature*
>   *weeps,*
> *If night could say how many eyes are fixed*
> *On her dark shadows, while creation sleeps!*

The blue light of my phone gives me a headache. The day slides into dawn.

The hospital again, the staircase, the waiting room; a chair by the window, the rack of leaflets on the wall. The women with gypsy-style headscarves, or attached to IV drips; the occasional solitary man. Another young woman sitting stricken with her silent mother. My name is called. Everything you take for granted may yet be overturned.

And suddenly it's over. There is a name for it, and it's not exactly common, but it's benign. You can go, they say. Come back six months after you finish breastfeeding, or at most a year from now, and we'll re-examine you to be on the safe side. They've changed the boxes on the form so the Registrar can't find which one to tick, and then she does, and then it's done, the flimsy white paper to the ground floor receptionist and out of there, into the merciless, beautiful, stultifying heat. I will make my life matter, I promise to the day. I will use my voice. I will fight for what is right. The promises well up in me. I will spend less time on social media. I will not take my husband for granted. I will never snap at my children again. My children. I will teach them that it's their job, too, to make a difference. I will try to be a good example. I will. I will.

Back in 1863, Caroline finishes a novel in which her heroine refuses to bow to shame. Beatrice Brooke is seduced and then abandoned by the rich, predatory Montague Traherne; alone in Wales, her illegitimate baby boy dies. But Beatrice rebuilds her life: she sells her drawings and handmade lace, she moves back to London, becomes an artist's model. Against all odds and social conventions, *Lost and Saved* has a happy ending: Beatrice marries and has another child. This time, the reviews are split. Some call it a work of 'true genius', her best to date, but others are offended that a fallen women could be so redeemed. Caroline defends her heroine in the Letters pages of *The Times*, then starts work on her next and final novel, although of course she does not yet know it will be her last. Her middle son, *in a dreadful echo of my youth*, becomes increasingly violent; his wild and capricious moods taking dark turns. He flies into irrational rages and blames her for things that are not her fault, so that she is afraid to see him and hides in her room. He shoves her about and tells her to get out of his sight. He berates her in foul language. He hits her, and he hits his wife.

We go on. We endure, and go on. The old battles, the same battles, once again and in endlessly new configurations. On the 24th July it is announced that the inflatable baby will travel to Sydney for the forthcoming US Presidential visit there. RAICES tweets a plea to its followers:

@RAICES | 7:53 PM, 25 Jul 2018

Keep this in mind:

Children are still in cages. Parents still don't know where their children are.

Some were coerced illegally into leaving the country.

The media isn't writing as many stories but the problem has not gone away.

Please, don't let up.

Ghillie's Mum

Lynda Clark

WHEN HE WAS A baby, Ghillie's mum was mostly an orangutan. Like most mothers, she'd cradle him in her arms and blow raspberries on his belly, but unlike most mothers, she'd also change his nappy with her feet. In those early days, as far as he could recall, it was only at bath time she was other animals. A baby elephant to squirt him with water from her trunk, a porpoise to bat his rubber duck around the bath with her domed head, a dumbo octopus making him laugh with her big, flapping earlike fins, and grasping his bath toys with her many arms.

Ghillie assumed everyone's mother was many things, and so didn't worry about it at all for the first few years of his life. But when he started school, he realised his mum wasn't like other mums. And that meant he wasn't like other kids.

'Your mum had sex with a pig!' said Caspar, a boy in Ghillie's year, but far larger and with much harder fists. 'That's why she's all animals.'

Ghillie asked his mum about it when he got home. He didn't really know what sex was, and he was worried it might make her cross if he asked, so he just parroted Caspar's statement to her and asked if it was true.

'Isn't it nice that he thinks I'm *all* animals?' she said. 'I'm not even sure I can do them all myself.' And she became a fat little Shetland pony and gave Ghillie rides around their living room, making the worn carpet worse than ever with her hooves. Ghillie kept the taunts to himself after that, because she didn't seem to understand anyway.

★

Parents' evening made the situation difficult to ignore. It was autumn and dark early, so Ghillie's mum was a panther, prowling alongside him, amber eyes mindful of danger. She led him over the crossing and up to the school gate, weaving through the assembled parents and children who'd stopped to chat on the playground before going in. Ginny McClaren's mum screamed, and Ghillie's mum bared her teeth in response. Caspar elbowed his dad and they both stared, lips curled.

'Please, Mum,' said Ghillie, and she became a racoon by way of apology as they went inside.

★

'I've had some concerns about Ghillie's language development,' said Mrs Rodney, Ghillie's English teacher. 'Although I think now I see the root of the problem.'

Mum was sitting on her tail on the little plastic chair, scratching her furry belly with her small black hand-paws.

'Mrs Campbell! Would you at least do me the courtesy of being human while we speak?'

Mum became a naked, sad-faced woman, with dark rings around her eyes. 'It's Ms,' she said. Her hair was long and covered her breasts, and she drew one leg up against her chest to hide herself further, but several parents had noticed and were covering their children's eyes. Mrs Rodney was scandalised. She took off her cardigan and made Ghillie's mum put it on.

'I think it's time social services were involved,' Mrs Rodney said firmly.

★

Social services gave Mum a whole list of conditions she had to adhere to. She wasn't allowed to be animals anymore, under any circumstances. She could no longer work as what she called an 'occupational therianthropist' (Ghillie didn't know what that part meant) and instead had to get a real job where she contributed to society. If she didn't, they would take Ghillie away from her. She nodded, her mouth a thin line, unlike any animal Ghillie had seen.

★

Ghillie's speech didn't get any better. If anything, it grew worse. He didn't have much to say to the tall, wan woman who made him porridge in the mornings, and returned from work each day greyer and greasier, smelling of chips.

'Can you not bring chips home sometimes?' asked Ghillie one day.

Mum shook her head. 'We have to throw them away at the end of the shift,' she said. 'You wouldn't want them anyway.'

'Why not?'

'The potatoes are old, diseased things, coated in grease to make them seem better.'

★

The next parent's evening was different and the same. Mum washed her hair, but it was still greasy and lank. It was like that all the time now. She wasn't animals anymore, not even when she was getting ready. Ghillie used to love that, when she crawled into her nightshirt as an otter, and then transformed, arms sliding out of the sleeves like buds growing. But on this day, she just buttoned her shirt with her boring human fingers and told him she hoped he'd been behaving. She put on flared jeans and a sheepskin waistcoat, and licked her hands to slick down Ghillie's hair.

When they made their way through the school gate, Caspar elbowed his dad, who snorted, saying: 'What is this, the seventies?' and several of the other parents laughed.

Mrs Rodney was different, though. Solemn, polite, concerned.

'Ghillie barely speaks at all now,' she confided, as if Ghillie wasn't there and didn't know. 'Does he speak at home?'

Mum was perched on the tiny plastic chair, knees almost to her shoulders, all awkward human angles. She shrugged.

'When he has something to say.'

'And you don't have anything to say at school, Ghillie?'

Ghillie's eyes felt too big for his head. He worried for a moment that he was becoming an owl, but Mrs Rodney just continued to stare at him patiently. Mum reached over and squeezed his hand, and he shook his head.

'Very well,' said Mrs Rodney, but she didn't look like anything was very well at all.

★

That summer, Mum ended up in hospital. She slipped and poured hot fat all over herself at the chip shop. As she hit the ground, she became a pangolin and rolled up tight to avoid the worst of the searing liquid. Her boss said it was unhygienic to be an animal in a food place, no matter what the reason, and he couldn't let her work there anymore.

'Will they take me away?' Ghillie asked, sitting on a big plastic chair by her hospital bed, legs dangling, not reaching the floor.

'No, no,' said Mum, reaching for him with her big bandaged mitt.

And she was right.

They took her away.

★

People assume all kinds of things about you when you're silent. That you're stupid. That you're smart. That you can't hear. That you can't communicate. That it's a religious thing. That it's an attention-seeking thing. Over the years, Ghillie heard them all. The religious thing was closest to the mark, although truth be told, his motives were far from holy. He made a vow to speak only when he had something worth saying, but he persisted with it because of how crazy it made people. Social workers, teachers, policemen, doorsteppers, they couldn't bear his silence. Sympathy turned to rage in a surprisingly short space of time, particularly if he didn't meet their eyes. It gave him a perverse sense of pleasure, saying nothing as they wheedled and cajoled, pleaded and threatened.

The Registry wasn't so bad once he got used to it. The dorms were noisy at night, and some of the boys tried to taunt him into saying something, but at least he didn't have to put up with Mum's cat hairs on the pillow, and there were never stray feathers floating in his soup. The dorm warden was a kind man with large strong hands and deep pockets that bulged with bags of peppermints and chocolate-covered fudge and jelly snakes. The peppermint taste got into all the other sweets, but it was still preferable to fur and feathers.

The warden never asked Ghillie to speak either, just ruffled his hair and gave him a sweet. The warden had an old black labrador, and, the first time Ghillie saw it, he half-hoped it was his mother being sneaked in to visit, but of course it wasn't – she was in the Facility, probably for good. Unless she could stop being animals, which, of course, she couldn't.

★

Ghillie only visited her once during those years at the Registry. The warden took him. The Facility wasn't as nice as the Registry. Everything was painted pale lemon, intended to be clean and bright, but looking anaemic and sick. The foyer was nice, with red leather armchairs and a spiky green plant and a coffee table heavy with glossy hardcover picture books. But the foyer was separated from the rest of the Facility with a heavy door, a door that required the nurse to punch in a code on a keypad, before heavy bolts hissed back and it slid open. More of these doors separated the rest of the Facility's inmates from one another, and from the world.

Mum was on a chair in the middle of a room with no other furniture except an identical empty chair opposite. The floor was tiled, white with non-slip ridges. The warden indicated the chair for Ghillie and then retreated to the corner with the nurse and a cardboard cup filled with coffee. As Ghillie approached the empty chair, he saw there was a circular drain right in the centre of the room. Very strange.

Mum's hair had gone from lank to dry, the

ends split, wiry greying tangles tumbling to her shoulders over thin grey scrubs. She looked like an origami woman trying hard to stay folded.

She glanced up briefly as Ghillie sat down, gave him a twisted half smile and then became, very suddenly, a full-grown rhinoceros. The speed and force of the transformation knocked Ghillie, chair and all, over onto his back. As he struggled to sit up, she was quickly a woman again, her papery clothes shredded, but the nurse was already rushing towards her.

'I'm sorry!' Mum shouted. 'Ghillie, I didn't mean –' and then became a bird of paradise and swooped towards the ceiling, the plumes of her tail unfurling.

Ghillie couldn't respond, could only lie on the floor, rubbing the deep ache in the small of his back where the chair had butted into him. He stared at the odd guttering that skirted the room, scooped out hollows to guide non-existent liquids towards the central drain. The nurse tried to grab Mum, but she flew high, then swooped at the viewing window, smacking against the mirrored glass. She dropped to the floor, human and sobbing.

'It's these meds, it's these damn –' and she was a tiger, reddish orange and raging, but the nurse seemed unfazed and plunged a huge needle into the striped neck, pressing down on the syringe until it was empty. Even as she lapsed into unconsciousness, Mum continued to change, a mouse, a dog, a rat, a pigeon, a rooster, a chimpanzee, a trout, on and on, faster and faster, until they blurred together, a grotesque quivering mass of fins and fur and beak. As the orderlies wheeled her away and she continued to change weight and mass, Ghillie heard the gurney groan and squeak until they had disappeared through enough heavily locking doors. He was shocked and horrified. He'd never seen her like that before.

Maybe she could do all the animals.

'You see why we can't really have them in the community?' the nurse told the warden over Ghillie's head.

'What did she mean?' Ghillie asked and heard the warden's sharp intake of breath. That was one of the gifts of silence. When you spoke, it was a moment. 'About her meds?'

The nurse looked uncomfortable for a second, then placatory.

'If she takes her inhibitors consistently, then everything's fine. If she forgets, or refuses… there are side effects.'

Why couldn't she just take her inhibitors? Ghillie thought, even though he didn't know what inhibitors were.

★

When Ghillie turned eighteen, the warden bought him a cake and decked the top with candles in little plastic holders. It was a celebration of his birthday, but also a goodbye party, marking the end of his time at the Registry. He didn't know where he would go when he left at the end of the day, but they'd given him a rucksack and a change of clothes and some money, so he supposed it would be all right.

All the Registry's current charges came to see him blow out his candles, the youngest around seven, the oldest due to leave herself in a month's time. Ghillie stared at the candles, watching the wax dribbling down towards the cake's iced surface, wondering if it was still good to eat if the wax got on there. The other charges sang the leaving song, but the warden didn't join in. His arms were folded, gaze fixed on the cake.

Ghillie drew in a deep breath, planning his exhale carefully so it was powerful enough to extinguish the candles, but didn't expel any spit, because everyone should get a share of the cake, and they wouldn't want it with his spit all over it. But then he was a wolf, and instead of exhaling over the cake, he howled at the ceiling, a long, mournful noise, louder than any he'd ever made as a human.

The seven-year-old screamed, but the warden told him to shut up, SHUT UP, and that it was time for Ghillie to go now, and he helped Ghillie get his front legs through the straps of the rucksack as if Ghillie were still a person and ushered him outside, closing the door behind them on the hubbub of shocked children. He put his arms around Ghillie's neck like Ghillie had seen him do with the Lab, and he whispered in Ghillie's large ear: 'Don't let them put you in the Facility. You don't need to be in there.'

And Ghillie wished he had his human voice so he could thank the warden for everything, but he didn't, so instead he licked the salt tears from the warden's cheeks and ran off into the winter dark.

★

'Daddy, can't we come and see Nanny too?' Rocha was a marmoset, and her sister, Bri, for reasons known only to herself, was a huge ox, licking cereal out of her bowl with a long mobile tongue, tail swishing like a metronome, large bovine eyes glued to the cartoon channel. Rocha dangled from Bri's horn, and once again Ghillie felt proud and jealous that they had mastered their gift so young. He could still only force out a few words while he was animal, and his mum had never got the hang of it.

Ghillie buttoned his shirt.

'No kiddos, Nanny doesn't need you two tromping around.'

Juhn was out front, mowing the lawn. It was early spring, and it didn't really need doing yet, but she got a little frustrated sometimes when the kids insisted on being animals all day. Firstly, breaking up a fight between a kangaroo and a Komodo dragon wasn't a fun way to spend a Saturday, and second, she'd told Ghillie in the confessional space beneath their duvet one night, she often felt like the odd one out, the boring human.

'If you could have this, would you?' Ghillie had asked. 'Would you really?'

And she'd looked him in the eye and said, 'Yes' with such conviction it reaffirmed for him that she was the right one, forever.

He pulled her away from the lawnmower and kissed her hair. 'If they get too much, just spray them with the hose.'

'Even in the house?'

'Even in the house,' he confirmed, turning back to her as he reached the gate. 'Kids are water resistant!'

★

She was an elderly polecat, curled up in a wicker chair, brown mask flecked with grey. All her animals were old now. Ghillie picked up a photo from her dresser. It was the Home's last gala day. All the residents were in the swimming pool, and in the centre Mum was a dolphin and everyone was smiling.

They had both been uncertain about the Home at first, fearing it was another version of the Facility, just with floral throw pillows and baskets of pot-pourri to veil the smell of formaldehyde. But there was no formaldehyde here, and no locked doors, apart from at night and that was just because Mr Gibson was a nudist absconder.

As Ghillie put the photo back on top of the chest of draws, she woke and became an aged python. She draped herself around his neck by way of greeting, then slid over to the bed and under the covers to become human, because even the most open-minded son would rather not see his eighty-year-old mother naked if it could be avoided.

'I've been practising something,' she told him. Her hair was snowy white now, though not as white as the owl Juhn had found snagged in a barbed wire fence all those years ago, wing broken and bleeding.

'Have you?' Ghillie sat down in her arm chair, and leaned back. How shocked Juhn had been when the vet had told her: 'Actually, it's not an owl, it's one of them.' And then double-shocked, when he had whispered in an aside: 'I could put it down for you if you like? Pretend we didn't realise?' And she'd rushed out of there with the half-conscious creature in a cardboard pet-carrier and taken him home and waited for him to be a person again.

Ghillie's mum became a rabbit, nose twitching. Became human again. 'No, that's not right.' Ghillie waited as she became a miniature pig. He'd never understood how she could do such a range of animals. The kids could do it too, from vole to crocodile and back again with ease. He had to build up to something large, and even then, it was hard to hold. No shape was hard to hold for them, his daughters, his mother. Back as an old, old, lady, she pulled the covers up to her chin and grimaced in frustration. 'That's not it either. I'm sorry Ghillie, I'm becoming a useless old woman.'

'Becoming?' asked Ghillie with one eyebrow raised. She threw a pillow at him.

Juhn had told Ghillie off when he came out of his snow-owl delirium and described the transformation as 'becoming a person'. 'You're always a person,' she'd said. 'Whether you're a donkey, or a gibbon, or, I don't know, a naked mole rat, you're never not a person.' That conviction, even back then, before she knew him. And then the law was repealed, and so the state saw him that way too, a person. There were still plenty of people who didn't see him as a person, but their power was waning.

And just as he thought that, lying on the bed was a dragon, not a komodo dragon, an actual dragon, with lustrous copper-coloured scales and golden eyes and horns and a frilled ruff of thorny scales around her throat. She opened her mouth and for a moment Ghillie thought she was going to burn him up, that she hadn't really forgiven him for abandoning her, that these last few wonderful years had just been her biding her time until she could get her revenge.

But instead she said: 'Pudding.' And collapsed back into a tired old woman.

'Pudding?' asked Ghillie.

'I said a word,' she said indignantly, pulling on her robe just so she could put her hands on her hips and glare at him. 'I said a word as an animal. You were so impressed when the girls did it, I thought I'd try it.'

'The dragon was impressive!' said Ghillie, and moved onto the edge of her bed and hugged her, laughing. 'You realise that when the girls hear about this they're not going to leave you alone until you do a unicorn?' He didn't think he'd ever hugged her with both of them human before. It was strange. She was soft, fragile, breakable, just like him.

And Juhn was right, in a way, but she had it backward. They were never not animals, Ghillie and his mum, and that was the right way for them to be.

Silver Fish in the Midnight Sea

Jacqueline Crooks

MUMA'S FOETAL-CURLED LIKE dem white crick-necked flowers in the garden's sunken flower bed; their silvery hairs deflecting heat.

She works nights at the old people's home, six days a week. She's gotta sleep in the day. But the cussed summer light and heat's messing with her. Laying in that boxy bedroom of hers, frowsy with ganja smoke and sticky-sweet body heat.

She'll be drifting soon, spliff burning. Dreaming she's buried in the garden with termites and millipedes crawling over her face, leaving slime and white powder trails. Dream-travelling back to the starfish island she came from fifteen years ago. An island that erupted from sea crust millions of years ago. Raining nightfall ash.

We live in an old pebble-dashed house on a housing estate in a city south-east of this bone-grey island where Muma's lived since she was eighteen.

Muma yells the drill on Day One of the summer holiday:

'Ycara, Macca, Carlos – come yah!'

We children step – quick-time.

'Oooonuh mus' not be seen. Not heard.' She slams the metal gate that opens to the dead-end street; bolts it top and bottom. Flings me one of her sting-fe-touch looks.

'Keep de pickney in the yard,' she tells me, before she slow-times it back inna the house.

Locked in. Locked out. Three bendy-boned, streggae-streggae children left to ramp in the garden. I've gotta keep my brother and sister quiet, morning, noon and night, so Muma can sleep.

Day Two of the summer holiday and Sound-Ghost's winding all over me – a strangling vine strung with bitter berry eyes, watching me standing on the chair, trying to unbolt the rusty lock from the top of the kitchen door. A kitchen of wooden shelves lined with old newspapers, stacked with tins of cocoa beans and musty island herbs. Blackened stove in the corner and a grave-size enamel sink by the window.

We're allowed out through the kitchen back door that leads into the garden where bushes and trees make island-shaped shadows on the ground.

Lemon light; air fizzing with insects. Elderberries swarming like a disease across the zinc fence.

No way Sound-Ghost is coming inna the garden. Sound-Ghost prefers the blooming black spores on the damp walls of our house where her memories are.

'Come, nuh' I shout. Macca and Carlos come wid bruck-neck speed and we're standing on the red, polished backdoor step like we're getting ready to dive inna the sea.

I shuub Macca and Carlos out – out inna the overgrown garden, with dead yellow grass stacked like the straw houses of before-time people from Muma's starfish island.

I watch Macca and Carlos in their too-tight polyester tank tops and denim shorts – bare-footed, open-mouthed, soaking their bones in sunlight.

My sister and brother have got the same black whorl afros, coral-brown skin, noses broad as portholes but they're as different as Sound-Ghost and Muma. Carlos is six. Macca is eleven, four years younger than me. Mahena Anita Caye Ayiti

Macca – she has more names than any of us put together, and more attitude.

No photos of her as a baby. Macca was sent to an aunt and uncle on Muma's starfish island when she was a baby, 'cos Muma's mind had turned to clay.

Macca pops up outta nowhere when she's three, like that photo in Muma's burgundy, gold-lettered album which, years later, I'm staring at with my big self, tracing my finger around her blurred face. A three-year-old with frizzy plaits standing on a beach at night. She has red eyes where the camera flash has found a pool of red at the back of her eyes.

The sunken flower bed is the centerpiece of the overgrown garden, created by Mr Adler, who used to live in our house with Sound-Ghost when she was his wife. The Council told Muma, when they housed us, that Mrs. Adler left Mr Adler; just disappeared one day. The council moved Mr Adler into the sheltered flats on the other side of the garden. They said the house was a family house and he was on his own.

He begged to be close to his garden. Said it took him eight years to get it the way he wanted it. Everything flowering and dying when *he* wanted it to.

And, bwoy, you couldn't get closer to our garden than those sheltered flats. We never saw anybody except Mr Adler. The only things moving in that old people's block were steam from small kitchen windows, smells of piss and gas and cabbage, and dem terrace lights that glowed blue in the day and red in the evenings.

'Dem send him there fe dead,' Muma said. 'No step foot ovah deh!' She warned.

Mr Adler's flat is on the third floor. I see him most days leaned-up against the balcony, smoking, eyes digging up his garden. Watching us. The way Muma's island ancestors watch us from the night sky with their shark eyes.

For a long time, I believed that Muma and Sound-Ghost were the same person. That Sound-Ghost was really Muma, speaking to me through her spirit, cos her body died when she sent Macca away. But Sound-Ghost and Muma ain't one and the same. Sound-Ghost nevah came from no Caribbean island like Muma's. They're as different as mudstone and shale.

Muma's trying to go deep inna sleep.

Sound-Ghost's trying to rise up again. She wants to mek noise like us. She wants to be seen. A ghost trying to mek her way back. Hungry for touch.

I call her Sound-Ghost cos she's always humming dem new ghost sounds, trying to speak. Feeding on furred-up memories from our haunted house – the house she used to live in.

I'm the only one can see her. True seh my sight is different. I kept my eye on Macca when she was sent away. Four years watching my sister from far. My eyes became chambers of sound and heat. Time messes up when you use your eyes that way. You see things from the past, the now, and times to come.

I stay on the doorstep with Sound-Ghost. 'G'lang,' I tell Macca and Carlos, 'but nah bother mek up noise.'

They run crazy around the garden as if they're going places that only they can see: hiding in the tall grass; stamping through it; running around the edges of the garden, panting. At the back of the garden, feathery plants stand talawa against the metal fence like island ancestors, guarding entry to the underworld. Island underworld where ancestors with mashed-in-skulls watch us, swinging baskets of polished bones, telling us, '*Come.*'

Dem people no easy.

Carlos is jumping up and down on the sunken flower bed, some made-up ancestor dance. 'Aeejaaaahh, Aeeejaaah,' he shouts. Macca is pulling at the fence like she's trying to get out.

Sound-Ghost, smelling of mould and summer haze, winds herself tighter around me. I step into the garden and she disappears.

Mr Adler is watching Macca.

He stubs his cigarette out on the rail. Twists and turns it. Smoke coming outta his bad-breath mouth.

'Ease off the fence!' I say to Macca.

She looks at me, dem eyes o' hers hard as cocoa beans.

'Muma's outta it, always smoking weed,' she says.

I put my finger to my lips. 'You know too much.'

'Never be heard. Cha!' she says. 'Not be seen? We're like duppy.'

'Don't speak dem ways!' I say.

I feel too much; Macca knows way more. But there's no time to worry about Mr Adler. I need to keep the children quiet. Because Muma's gotta go deep inna sleep. Like unborn pickney.

I go in the kitchen. Sound-Ghost is memory-guzzling in the stone larder. Sniffing her old life from the smell of rot, rat shit and cigarette butts.

Humming so 'til I ask her, 'What!'

She can't speak; she's locked outta the world like we three. But it's more than that, 'cos now she's winding around me like she wants to get inna my body.

'Rest yourself,' I tell her and she's gone again.

I mix strawberry powder with cream, dash in brown sugar. Drizzle condensed milk over a bowl of broken ginger biscuits. I sit with Macca and Carlos on the stone step of the back door that faces the garden. We drink from yellow plastic cups that smell of elastic bands. Eat, suck sugar off our fingers.

Mr Adler waves. Carlos waves back. Macca shades her eyes, looks at him.

'What dat old man want?' she says.

A breeze cuts through the grass and the big old plum tree rains seeds and pollen. The sun moves behind a cloud and the garden slides to grey.

I hear the ancestors in the breeze, chanting: '*Come.*'

We pretend we don't hear children playing in the street, riding their bikes around the grass-inlaid roundabout.

Carlos is kneeling on the sunken flower bed that's six inches below the rest of the garden – a rectangular shape edged with black slate.

'Gonna get treasure,' he says. He's dug up three rusty hair grips and a lace handkerchief clotted with snails and pellet shit. He's placed them side by side on the ground.

'Leave dem dead people's things,' Macca tells

him. 'Digging up death like that!' She kicks dirt over them, tries to shuub them back inna the earth, kicking and stamping until there's sweat on the tip of her nose.

Sound-Ghost is in the kitchen singing high-arsed notes – some crazy zaggedy hum – but her ghost words won't come. The strings have been cut from her throat.

I look up to the sky to see where the sun's gone. I look for ancestor stars, but they'll come later, like silver fish in the midnight sea.

'Come, do stars,' I say to Macca. Her skin's a shade darker than it was couple hours ago – terracotta, underlain with gold.

She lays her head in my lap, I put my hand backa her head. The flat bones opening and closing in my hands. A conch shell.

I work quick, 'cos this girl don't like to be touched. She came back to us from Muma's island all strange. Fired up.

I aim the tweezers at her left eye, pluck a silver star from the lash on the outer corner. The star squirms. I squash it between my fingernails and wipe my hands on my green cotton flares. I pluck all the stars I can see. I put the tweezers into her ear. Clear the sand from her head.

'Why she got sand inna her head,' Carlos asks.

'Cos of Muma's island,' I say.

'I'm from the bottom of nowhere,' Macca says.

I put my hand on her heart. It's got a riddim like the metallic dribble of dem island tunes that Muma plays Sunday nights when we're in bed. Muma and Sound-Ghost, nodding their heads when island tunes lick them in the guts.

'I belong to me,' Macca says, pushing my hand away, back-slapping the air like she's hitting a ghost.

And my heart's busting, 'cos I can see she's mekking her way outta here again, staring beyond the fence and the greenest grass on the other side. Grass green as those places in the Psalms where people walk and don't 'fraid death.

Beyond the fence, the grass running around the old people's flats; a path of bruck-up tiles that looks like a lightning strike, cutting straight through the green out onto Lakeland Street, to the high street. Beyond that, the red-bricked building of the Palace Swimming Baths where freed children are swimming underwater in bleach-blue cold water. Diving and coming up with white pearls in their eyes.

Muma doesn't want us in dem places, playing with dem children 'Cos this cold place isn't my island,' she says. 'Me no know these people.'

'Muma should go back to her island,' Macca says.

I look inna my sister's eyes – clear as water – the faces of Muma and Carlos reflected somewhere in the distance.

My face isn't there. I'm here still. And always. I'm here three years from now in one of the corrugated roof garages that are lined up on the northern flank of the garden. Splayed on the back seat of an old car. Some dibby-dibby man thrusting his dead weight eyes inna me.

I'll go anywhere if you take me away.

The dibby-dibby man ain't going anywhere. All he can say is: *It's just you and me, baby.*

He's pulling my hair and yanking my head back and my voice is exploding out of me.

Day Seven of the summer holiday. Sunday, three o'clock, seaside heat. Macca sitting on the parched earth, leaning against a stack of dead grass. Her face heart-coloured. Nostrils pumping. Carlos is pulling pink petals from the rose bush and mixing them with water from the plastic cup.

'Perfume for Muma,' he says. He's the baby and Muma's the centre of his world.

The garden is the centre of Mr Adler's world. He comes to our house every couple of weeks to check for mail. He comes when there are grey rock clouds in the sky – tall and bowed as a dowsing rod, walking down the road; buttoned-up to his neck in a black trench coat, two black craters where his cheekbones shoulda been.

Muma keeps him standing on the doorstep, the door pulled behind her so he can't see how life's treating her. 'Yes, Mr Adler. How life treating *you*?'

We crouch on the other side of the door.

'Garden's choked dry,' Mr Adler says.

I move forward, see his sliver-wet lips, his arms swinging at his sides like sharpened machetes.

'Look 'pon me, Mr Adler,' Muma says. 'Pickney. Work. Cook. Clean. Who-and-who have time to be digging up any rag-tag garden?'

'I'd come once a week. Left my tools in the shed. Don't want to bother you with my handiwork...'

'Give the neighbours plenty to chat 'bout, Mr Adler. Me and my children stand out as it is. Only black family on this estate. We confuse dem: Black blood, Indian blood – every kinda Caribbean blood. Me? Me keeping me head down, Mr Adler. Outta sight, outta mind. That's how we must live.'

'Think about it. You never know.' He pauses, leans in like he's trying to see inside. He sees Macca crouching at the door; smiles one o' dem 'better than yuh' smiles, puts his hand near her face, like's he's gonna touch her. He holds his hand close to her face for a second then asks, 'Letters?'

'None, Mr Adler.' Muma slams the door; turns on us. 'Man should know when to let go. *Let it go!*'

And I'm not sure if Muma's saying that he should let go of Sound-Ghost or the garden or the house or his letters – which she hides in her underwear drawers.

Muma acts like she's possessed when she's angry. Maybe it's just anger about the men that come and go.

'Don't like that man,' Macca says when we're in the garden. 'Like dem bug-eyed men on Muma's island. Crawling everywhere.'

Macca is chasing Carlos with the garden fork from the shed. 'Run, escape,' she shouts.

He's trying to dodge her but she's quick; springing on the tips of her toes from one side to the other, poking his arms with the garden fork.

'Leave me!' Carlos shouts. His small fists curled tight like marbles.

There's rapping on the upstairs window. Muma's face is pressed against the glass – her red headwrap on her head like a spear tip.

She flings open the window. 'Get oonuh backside up here now!'

I drag Macca and Carlos upstairs to Muma's room. Macca's kicking and throwing punches.

Carlos' eyes are wide but he's quiet.

Muma pulls them into her bed. 'Yuh mus' sleep 'cos me mus' sleep, to work and feed yuh,' she says.

She covers them in the thick, scratchy, pink fleece blanket.

They lie on their backs, staring up at the ceiling.

Macca throws the covers off. 'Even ghosts get to play,' she cries.

'Play? Play?' says Muma. 'What me evah know 'bout play?'

Muma lashes her legs with her hands five times. 'I. Will. Give. You. Play. I will give you ghosts.'

Carlos cries like he's the one that's been beaten.

Macca stares at the corner of the room, squinching away the tears.

'Go clean the kitchen,' Muma tells me.

Last I see, Sound-Ghost's crying dust and sand into Macca's eyes.

It's six o'clock and Muma's coloured herself in for work. She wears a denim skirt with a burgundy tassel belt and turquoise platform shoes. We're sprawled on the floor, cooling ourselves on the black slate tiles.

'Jus' three hours of sleep,' Muma says. She's beyond tired, the whites of her eyes embroidered in red; black cross-stitches around sucked-in lips. 'Now fe work me backside off.' She swings her bag over her shoulder. 'No answer the door. No care who-and-who it is.'

True seh Muma is a shine-faced beauty. Black hair in a beehive. Black waves defying gravity. Little to no sleep, but she's gonna work the ten-hour night shift at Carlton House, wet-rag-slapping maaga old people on white beds.

'Keep that back door shut,' she says. 'Keep yuh arses inside. Me no want no mad man inna my yard.'

She slams the front door.

But her energy's still here. Vibrating heat and sadness.

I fry mincemeat in pepper sauce; toss in yesterday's turned cornmeal.

We eat on the floor, listening to the radio crackling with old church songs, sermons, and weather forecasts of summer gales.

An unusual Atlantic low-pressure system. Brutal winds.

I wash the dishes. The light in the garden changes from ochre to crimson.

Sound-Ghost, near the stone larder, is sucking on crepey dust, trying to vibrate into mass. Into matter.

Nothing matters, but that Muma mus' sleep. A sleep that takes her down through rocks, clay, chalk, sand, and streams, and the ancestor bones in-between.

I pull the back door, swollen with heat and moisture. It scrapes the tile floor.

I run out.

'Us too!' Macca shouts. She and Carlos are on the doorstep.

'Come, nuh.'

The plum tree's like a fat incense stick. We're safe under the branches that are coated in rotting sugar fungus.

Mr Adler is not on the balcony.

Light breeze, puppet-bobbing plants. Macca lights a bundle of dried grass. We inhale the smoke, exhale the way Muma does, like ancestral island chiefs. Smoke and heat and we're high. Black clouds shaped like islands forming, burning, and dying in the sky.

'Tell us one of your duppy stories,' Macca says.

I spin it from the top: 'There's a volcano on the seabed. Made outta this woman's bones and her lava flowing blood. Her man buried her millions of years ago when the world was black-and-white silent.

Nothing stops her ash-flow breath. She erupts from the seabed, firing hot rocks and blood.

Carlos has fallen asleep, his head of black curls resting on my lap.

I pick him up, put him over my shoulder.

'Bed! Come on, you.' Macca looks at me and I see the red islands in her eyes; see this house three years from now, demolished; the earth turned over. Rotten tools. More bones. Skulls.

Carlos will go to another island. An island that's colder than this one in winter. A musician, sounding out his pain on a guitar. I'll go to Muma's starfish island where I've found the black sand place that Macca once lived, a wooden shack in the bush, in the path of a volcano. The aunt and uncle who cared for her long gone. I'm thin as a bag of bones. Hiking the plateaus that formed millions of years ago. Wondering how many *rahtid* years before eruptions cool.

I tuck Carlos into the bottom bunk. Macca's already on top. Her face pressed against the damp wall.

'Night.'

She sucks her teeth. 'Not be *seen*!'

I go downstairs and stand on the doorstep looking over at the old people's place. It's dark, and silver fish are swimming in the sky. Breeze blowing hard.

I push the door. It drags against the stone floor with a high-pitched squeal. I get it as close as I can inside the frame, but not close enough to fasten the bolt. Sound-Ghost beside me rasping death breath.

I go up to my room.

I'm deep inna sleep when the sound of the sea wakes me. It's the wind cussing through the long grass, the house creaking and moaning like an old ship.

I check the children. Carlos is lying on his back, eyelids flickering.

Macca is gone.

I run downstairs; see the kitchen door wind-butting against the frame.

Out inna the garden, *huracana* wind and rain, the feather-heads of the plants ripped off. Birds in the plum tree squawking and flapping.

The bushes are underwater caves.

Ancestors watching from the sky with shark eyes.

And I realise that it's Macca they've been watching. She's theirs.

I can't breathe.

'Macca!' I run to the back of the garden. The wire fence has been trampled at the far end. I step over it. Run, across the lawn of the old people's block. Smells of sweat and piss and duppy musk.

'Macca!'

Air spinning dread fast. Sounds of air and rain and screams. I look back. Black ash steaming out of the sunken garden; Sound-Ghost erupting from black crust, surging and screeching.

'Don't touch the child.'

But it's too late. Mr Adler is standing on his balcony. The rain jooking-up his face. He's looking straight at me. Through me. Beyond me. His face twisted like he's drowning.

I see Macca's spirit in the ash vibrations of Sound-Ghost's eruption. Mekking her way back. The way ghosts do. Vibrating. Beyond Mr Adler's touch.

Macca, rising up.

Afterglow.

My Beautiful Millennial

Tamsin Grey

1.

IT'S A FRIDAY HALFWAY through December, my day off from my shit job. I've got a cold, and would have languished in my lumpy, scratchy bed, but Paul Fildes has summoned me to Amersham. He wants to have a discussion about Christmas, but not over the phone, because he finds our phone calls impossible. When I fall silent, it's like I'm howling in pain, and he can't reach me.

I take ages getting dressed, i.e. even longer than usual. I have finally gone for my black velvet dress with the flouncy skirt, bottle-green tights and my lace-up boots. Amethyst lipstick. My strange curly hair in spikes. My Napoleon coat, black beret, black leather gloves. My green carpet bag, yes, the same green as my tights. Paul Fildes says I wear 'dressing-up' clothes, that it's a sign of my arrested development. He has offered to take me shopping, for a suit, blouses, interview clothes. It would be fun to try things on in classy boutiques instead of charity shops, but I'm trying to disentangle myself from Paul Fildes.

Leaving my room in disarray, I creep out of the house that I share with around five other humans. (As they're mainly invisible, I can't be more precise.) It's biting cold, with a rose-gold sun throwing long black shadows. I pick up my wages from Mingles, and head for Aldgate. Outside the station a man in a gold paper crown is holding out a white paper cup. He has decorated his dog with tinsel, and the dog is all agitated, shaking and pawing himself, trying to get the stuff off. I drop a twenty-pence piece into the man's paper cup. He frowns.

'Is that all you can afford, love?'

Totally thrown, I dig in my bag for the brown envelope I've just been given, which I know contains ten twenty-pound notes, which I'm planning to hand over to Paul Fildes, and two tenners, which need to last me a whole week.

'Joking!' He's laughing, putting his hand over mine, to stop me opening the envelope. I flee into the station.

The Metropolitan line is a maroon colour, and Paul Fildes and I are marooned on either end of it. The train is waiting, silent and stately. I'm the first one on, and it feels like I'm spying on a secret world. Each way, the walk-through carriages, on and on, repeating themselves, the yellow poles, the yellow nooses, and the black strips saying AMERSHAM, AMERSHAM, AMERSHAM. Amersham is the resting place of Ruth Ellis, the last woman in Britain to be hanged. I know this because the last time I went to Amersham, Paul Fildes took me to see Ruth's grave.

I cringe, and sit down, putting my bag on the seat next to me, and as I pull off my hat and gloves I remember the cup man's raw, chapped fingers, and cringe again. I kind of hate him, and hate myself for hating someone who's slipped through the cracks and hung onto his sense of humour. The train starts moving, and I gaze up at the yellow nooses, rehearsing my speech to Paul Fildes.

'You have been so kind…' 'You are a wonderful, generous person, and I know that…' 'Paul, I need to be straight with you…'

Paul Fildes is the only person I've got to know since I moved to London, which was in the spring, after I got the all-clear, and my hair more or less covered my head. I could have gone back to uni, but all my friends had already left, and it would have been too weird, starting all over again. I met him on a personal development weekend, which my mum paid for as my twenty-first birthday present. She left her job to look after me, and has hardly any money herself, so it was generous of her, but I so would have preferred the cash. There were about twenty people on the course. Paul Fildes stood out, being very tall and wide, with a great moon of a face, adorned with a bushy moustache. At the end, when everyone else was hugging and kissing, and I was standing there wondering if I was allowed to go home, Paul Fildes took me to one side and told me, very fervently, that he had a wealth of experience, and valuable contacts, and would like to support me to achieve my full potential.

'It's not that I don't like you…'

Do I like him? I think of his eyes, violet-coloured and thickly lashed, startling out of that great jowly face. On the personal development weekend he told everyone that his mother used to call him her 'little monster'. He also said that he was walking wounded from a relationship with a clinically depressed woman called Joy. He'd been a City boy, but had given that up because she needed twenty-four-hour attention. He'd supported her financially, through day trading, had carried her through five long years. He had got nothing back. It would be a long time before he was ready to risk intimacy again.

He wasn't anything like my idea of a City boy. But what did I know? On our first date – which I didn't realise was a date – he took me to the Dutch Pancake House in Holborn, and for a split second I was disappointed, but then decided it was an ironic place to have lunch. I hadn't drunk for a long while, so the house red went straight to my head. I didn't tell him about being ill, but I told him all my other secrets, including that I hated my mum's new boyfriend, that I was thinking of joining an escort agency, oh, and that I had voted Leave in the EU referendum.

He wasn't interested in my Brexit vote, said he hadn't bothered himself, as it wouldn't make any difference to people like him. I babbled on, telling him how I'd thought of leaving the EU as taking the road less travelled: as an adventure, a mystery, something wild and free. And then I'd realised that it was the opposite: that we were walling ourselves up, shutting things out; burying ourselves alive. I got carried away, half-knowing I was talking crap, and using my hands too much, until I knocked over my glass, and some wine dripped onto Paul Fildes' pale cavalry twill trousers. He tutted, and dabbed with his serviette, and said not to worry, these things happen. I passed him the water jug, and told him how nervous I was of people finding out, and thinking I must be a rustic racist.

'You live in fear of the vicious judgement of others.' He poured a drop of water onto the stain, shaking his head. 'Poor Dido.'

I laughed, feeling confused, and then asked why Brexit wouldn't affect people like him, and he put the jug down and said that he didn't want to talk about politics, he wanted to talk about us. And reached for my hand.

I snatched mine away. I was taken aback, because of what he'd said about needing to recover from Joy, and also because he is a lot older than me. But in a drunken muddle I wondered if I'd misread him, whether he was just being, I don't know, avuncular. Worried I'd been rude, I quickly passed him another serviette, trying to make it look as if that was why I'd moved my hand.

He said that he didn't think I should go into escorting. From what he understood of that industry, it wasn't just about going out to dinner. He looked hard at me to see if I'd got what he was driving at. I said that I wasn't under any illusions. He nodded, full of unspeakable emotion. To change the subject I asked him about day trading, and he groaned under his breath, and then asked for the bill. I asked what was wrong, and he suddenly exploded. 'Dido, you tell me you are going to prostitute yourself. And then you ask me about day trading. What am I meant to make of you?' I felt too upset to answer. Like I'd blown it, that he wouldn't want to have anything more to do with me. But once he'd paid, he seemed to pull himself together. He looked at his watch, and then out of the window, and gazed at me thoughtfully for a while. Then he said he hoped very much I would let him lend me some cash. It would be his pleasure, and he would be in no hurry to be repaid. 'I'm practically a baby boomer, Dido,' he said. 'And you' he said, reaching over and taking my jaw in his giant fingertips, 'are my beautiful millennial.'

I borrowed £200, and saw him a lot over the summer. He took me to the British Museum to see the mummies, to a very long foreign film at the National Film Theatre, and for a disgusting breakfast in the Best Western Hotel. I sent a snap of him to my friend Chloe, with the title *SUGAR DADDY*, but it wasn't like that. We kissed hello and goodbye (on the lips, mine firmly closed, his slightly parted). He never tried to take my hand again, but we brushed against each other surprisingly often. He would quiz me on whether I'd started therapy, or seen a spiritual healer, or written an angry letter to my mother, but I'd always failed to follow up any of his recommendations. He told me I was 'obstinate', 'evasive', 'complex', 'damaged', and also 'bewitching'. I took to teasing him, to lighten the mood, and to begin with he was perplexed, but he gradually understood, and one day he threw back his head and chortled. It was kind of like when a baby first laughs, apart from not, because, instead of joy and wonder, it filled me with a deep foreboding. He started trying to tease me back, but the best he could manage was these awful, priggish put-downs which made my blood run cold.

I kept seeing him, but I longed for people my own age, people who could do real banter, who knew who Ed Sheeran was and could discuss crisp flavours. In September, at his insistence, I trekked out to Amersham. His bungalow, on the edge of a cul-de-sac, smelt of socks and the remains of a kebab strewn under his two giant daytrading screens. There was one picture, a photograph of a ballerina. 'My mother,' he said, and hesitated, but said no more and I didn't like to ask. We got the bus to Old Amersham, which was all cobbles and timber, but with a Costa, and a Tesco's, and a Joules. In the graveyard he showed me where Ruth Ellis is buried. It's just a grassy patch with nothing marking it, and he told me how Ruth's son Andy destroyed the headstone with a hammer, just a few days before taking his own life. Andy had been ten when his mother was hanged, for shooting her racing driver lover dead outside the Magdala pub in Hampstead. As he told me about Andy, he reached for my hand again; paralysed by the sadness, I let him hold it.

2.

The pigeon gets on at Baker Street. I'm thinking about Paul Fildes, rehearsing what to say to him, and I haven't been following the starts and stops and comings and goings. I am vaguely aware of the teenager sitting opposite – that he's black, that he's dressed in black, with white trainers, and white wires coming out of his ears. And also the white woman doing her make-up, the way she's spread her kit out on the seat next to her, her silver fur coat, and her fountain of cream soda hair. I've taken in these two, and the bright red scarf of a man sitting further along, and a sad-eyed woman with a suitcase and two listless small children. I don't register the pigeon until it's right by my feet, bobbing and bustling, and I scream, I can't help it, and clutch my knees into my chest. And then I feel like a total idiot.

The boy opposite looks at me, and then the pigeon, and then back at his phone. No one else takes any notice, out of indifference, or politeness, who knows. I put my feet back down firmly, asserting myself over the pigeon. It's a battered-looking thing, lopsided, with petrol-sheened feathers and mangled feet. It holds its space, examining me first with one tiny orange eye and then the other. Trying to ignore it, I blow my nose, and then fix on the cream soda woman's application of mascara. It's weird, people doing their make-up on the tube. Such an interesting thing to watch, and they're doing it right there, right in front of you, but you feel like you should pretend it's not happening. Aware of the pigeon, I look at the man in the red scarf, a white man, peaky-looking, and he's wrapped the scarf across his nose and mouth like he's worried about breathing in germs. He looks familiar, but I don't know why. The ends of the scarf are tucked into his camel overcoat, underneath which he's wearing jeans and brown Chelsea boots. His legs are crossed, which is unusual for a man on the tube, and very thin, too thin to be wearing skinny blue jeans. I look back up at his face, and it dawns on me that he's a famous actor. I can't remember his name, but he might have been Dr Who for a while. As I study him, his eyes suddenly slide to meet mine, hostile, and I quickly look away. The pigeon seems to have moved closer, and my muscles tense, and completely by mistake, I look back at the actor, who notices, and I want to die. Everyone else is oblivious to him, even the listless children, because they are real Londoners, default setting 'Whatever', not wide-eyed Brexit-voting bumpkins like me. Then I realise that someone's talking, I can hear the sound of it but not the words and I see that it's the man in the orange puffer jacket. Guantanamo Bay orange, is what comes to me. He's partially hidden by the silver fur shoulder of the cream soda woman, so I can see a portion of the jacket, and his face, which is olive-skinned, his moving lips and his black curly hair. I watch his lips, trying not to remember that muttering is one of the signs of a suicide bomber. If I was a Londoner, I wouldn't be so jumpy, I wouldn't be so racist, I wouldn't be such a total jerk. But he's staring at his lap, and a fixed stare is another sign. Does he have a rucksack? I lean to my left, away from the pigeon, pretend to be looking in my bag. He doesn't have a rucksack, and he isn't just muttering to himself, but reading aloud from a book. He darts me a look, not hostile, questioning, and I fumble in my bag, pretending I didn't actually look at him at all. And then, as I straighten, the pigeon rushes at me head-long, and I scream again, and I flap my feet at it to ward it off, but the toe of my boot makes contact and, with a hoarse and terrible whistle, it rises a foot into the air and then plummets back to the floor.

'Fuck's sake…' The teenager pulls the plugs from his ears and peers at the pigeon. I notice the children looking too, with slack, incurious faces. The actor is looking at his fingernails.

'I'm so sorry,' I say to the boy.

'Don't say sorry to me.' The boy is watching the pigeon, which is back on its feet, but distinctly unsteady.

'I didn't. Do you think it's OK?'

The boy shrugs. Everyone gazes after the pigeon, who is pluckily hobbling up the aisle. Then the boy puts his earphones back in, and the reading man goes back to his book, and the celebrity sinks further into his scarf. It's only me watching the pigeon hobble along the train. I wonder if I should go after it, gather it up, pop it in my bag and take it to the nearest vet. How much would it cost, to mend a pigeon? Would the money in my bag be enough? The pigeon has turned around, is coming back, is picking up speed. I try to stay calm, to be in the moment; I close my eyes and listen to the reading man's lovely voice. But I know the pigeon is coming back to take revenge, and when I take a peek it's right there in front of me, its orange eyes blazing. And then, in a flurry of feathers it takes off, its beak aimed right at my face, and I jump up, lifting my arms, and break into a blind run. But someone's shouting after me, shouting, 'Madman! Madman!' and I've left my bag behind, so I stop and turn, my arms still covering my face. It's the reading man who's shouting, and he's waving, and beckoning, and pointing at the floor between us. Totally freaked out, I peer down and scream again, because it is the pigeon, dismembered, three pieces, the body and the two wings, flattened and somehow blackened, lying on the blue speckled floor.

And then I see that it's my hat and my two gloves, which had been on my lap, and the reading man is leaning over to pick them up. The pigeon doesn't seem to be anywhere, so I lower my arms. 'Thank you!' I take them from him, but I drop one of the gloves again, and we both go for it, nearly knocking heads. He gets to it first. 'Thank you!' I say again, and he smiles, and his eyes crinkle. His book is called *The Heart Is a Lonely Hunter* by Carson McCullers. I've heard of it, but I've never read it. 'I thought it was the pigeon.' I really wanted to explain that last crazy scream. 'I thought these were…' I hold up my hat and gloves, thinking he will never understand, that I should just pick up my bag and walk far away down the train. But the reading man is laughing, full of comedy and empathy. 'Yes, yes!' he says. 'You thought I was pointing at the pigeon.'

'Yes, but I thought that these were the pigeon. I thought…'

'Hah!' He laughs louder, nodding, totally getting it, he thinks it's hilarious, and suddenly I'm laughing too. And the children are laughing, and their sad-eyed mother is smiling, and the celebrity has lifted his chin out of his scarf and is grinning from ear to ear. And when I sit down, I see that the teenager is smiling, and I smile back at him, and he shakes his head, still smiling. And I just love him. I love everyone. Especially the reading man, who has gone back to his book with a smile still playing on his lips. The pigeon is wandering about, inspecting the floor, such a filthy, decrepit bird. I love that bird. I love its hardiness. I love its self-containment. I love the actor, who is a brilliant actor, if only I could remember his name. And I am very fond of the children, and their mother, who is talking to them both, probably about me, and stroking the little boy's hair. And that cream soda woman. What amazing hair. What an amazing coat. What amazing eyelashes – great shelves of black shadowing her neon-blue eyes. For the first time I notice an old Indian lady, an anorak over her sari, lots of shopping, battered Mary Janes. Her look is piercing. I smile at her, and she doesn't smile back. But that's just her way, it's absolutely fine. The train has come out of the tunnel and golden light is flooding in, and the reading man is reading aloud again, and though I still can't make out the words, it is so lovely, like I'm a child and he is reading me a bedtime story.

And the train arrives at Finchley Road; the actor stands up, the cream soda woman stands up and the reading man stands up, stuffing his book in his pocket, and as he steps out of the train he turns and lifts his hand. I lift my hand back, smiling and smiling, but then I see that the pigeon is walking round and round a yellow pole. 'You need to get off, pigeon!' I cry. The bird is very dear to me now, and I really don't want it to be trapped on the train all the way to Wembley Park. 'It's not going to get off!' I point at it. 'Someone needs to…' But no one moves. So I get to my feet and move towards it, waving my arms, trying to herd it out. I'm bold now, with the pigeon, I'm not frightened of it, I just want it to get off, but we run round and round the yellow pole like a couple of complete fools, and the reading man has stopped on the platform to watch. And then the beeping starts, meaning the doors are about to close, and I cry, 'Oh no!' I can't bear it. But at the very last second, the pigeon scurries between the doors and onto the platform, cool as a cucumber.

I watch the pigeon until I can't see it anymore, and then I go and sit down. And that's when the Indian woman starts talking to me.

'No need to worry about the pigeon.' She's leaning forward, hands on her knees, shouting over the roar of the train. 'The pigeon doesn't worry about you. Why should you worry about the pigeon?' I shrug and smile, but I feel tense again. She's not really having a go at me, it's just her way, but I want to cry. I get out my phone. On the screen, my friend Chloe kisses her new boyfriend, who is from Quebec, and very cute. Yearning twists my guts.

3.

The Indian woman gets off at North Harrow. I look out at the mysterious suburbs: the boxy houses, the pyramid roofs, the satellite dishes; a flash of a park, flat and green, a pair of goalposts, a deserted play area. I feel the melancholy weight of them, and my stomach turns over. I blow my nose and think back to holding hands over Ruth Ellis's grave. How, when I finally escaped back to the warm belly of the city, it came to me that I wasn't seeing Paul Fildes to relieve my own loneliness, but to relieve his. I ghosted him. Autumn turned into winter. I went for long walks along the river, all the way into town, looking at the lights on the water, listening over and over to the 'Heart of Glass' mash-up from *The Handmaid's Tale*. And then one day he turned up on my doorstep. I hadn't even realised he knew my address. To begin with he was stiff and angry, saying that I owed him £200, and I said I was very sorry and would pay him back within a week, if he would please give me his bank details. But then he sighed and said, 'Poor Dido. You look awful. I knew you must be ill.' And for some reason this made my eyes fill up, and he did that thing of taking hold of my jaw, tipping my face up so he could see into it, and I clenched my teeth and shook his fingers off. And he stepped over the threshold saying, 'Dido, Dido, why can't you bear anyone to look after you?' And one of the invisible humans came out of the kitchen to see what was going on, and I had to let him in, and up into my little room under the rafters, and it was like Alice when she ate the Eat Me cake; there just wasn't enough space for him. I was pathetic, mumbling that yes, I'd been depressed, and letting him explain to me about my trust issues. And then I let him hug me, and nuzzle at my neck. And it was all back on again, and coming up to Christmas. He hadn't made any plans, and was wondering if he could host his millennial waif. I would need to stay over on Christmas Eve because of the lack of transport. But he didn't want to rush me. He would sleep on the sofa. He paused, patting my knee, and then sighed and said, 'At least think about it.'

I imagine what would happen if I succumbed to Paul Fildes. Waking up on Christmas morning together, naked between his nylon sheets, he would kiss me, and call me his beautiful millennial. He would tell me there was no need to ever go back to the house in Mile End, and I would agree. I wouldn't be missed. Eventually the invisible humans would realise I had gone, and put my stuff into bin bags, and let the room to someone else, someone more able, more nimble, more 'London'. And I would become Mrs Fildes, and give the bungalow my feminine touch. I would no longer find him repellent but would cleave to him, like a pet. I would look out onto the cul-de-sac and, mid-afternoon, he might take a break from day trading to walk me around it. And when we got back in, I'd make us both a cup of tea.

4.

Trussed in navy Gore-Tex, he meets me off the train. 'Oh, poor Dido,' he says. 'You're full of cold.' I'd been thinking we'd just go for a coffee somewhere close to the station, but he wants to take me to a nice pub in Old Amersham. On the bus I go back to rehearsing the Christmas sentences in my head, but when I open my mouth I say that the most terrible thing happened on the train. I tell him about the pigeon, its deformed feet, and how I panicked in front of the other passengers. When I've finished he thinks for a while, biting his lip.

'You have told me that the pigeon terrified and repulsed you. Enough for you to lose control in front of strangers.' He shudders, and closes his eyes. I look out of the window, at a DIY shop called Chiltern Mica Hardware. 'It's about intimacy, isn't it?' He takes hold of my chin. 'Dido, is this your way of asking me to help you over your fear of intimacy?'

'No,' I say. 'I was telling you about a poor mangled pigeon, and how it freaked me out.' I get a flash of the reading man laughing, the crinkles round his eyes.

In the empty dining area of the pub a waitress is cleaning the tables with disinfectant so strong it makes my eyes itch. I can just hear Ed

Sheeran and Beyoncé singing together on the radio in the kitchen. He buys two glasses of house red, and asks if it ever occurs to me to ask him a question. I think of the ballerina, but I ask him whether he is still in touch with Joy, his ex-girlfriend, and how she's getting on. He looks puzzled, as if he can't remember who she is, and then says that she's fine. 'What, better?' I ask, and he says that she's made a full recovery, and has gone travelling.

I get out the money. 'What's that for?' he says.

'It's what I owe you,' I say. 'It was kind of you to lend me it.'

'But you can't afford to pay me back. You're broke.'

'I'm OK. I'll manage.'

'I don't want it.' He pushes it back at me, panicked. I stare down at the wad of notes. 'Dido, please,' he says. 'If you really want to pay me back, then spend Christmas with me.'

'No,' I say.

'Why?' he says.

'Because I don't want to see you anymore.'

I stand up, taking my coat off the back of my chair, and he tells me to sit back down, for goodness' sake. I say that I'm going, and he stands up too, and says he'll catch the bus with me. I say I'd prefer it if he didn't. When he tries to help me with my coat I push him away. The waitress looks over. He steps back.

'So you're paying me off,' he says.

'I'm paying you back,' I say.

'You're going off to be an escort.' I look towards the door.

'Well, I hate to be the one to tell you, Dido, but you're probably not pretty enough.' He nods, emphatic. 'You're too scruffy. Too grubby-looking. And your hair, my love, is terrible.'

I smile and leave the pub, lighter of step, a burden lifted. The bus is there at the bus stop, and I'm stepping onto it when he catches me up. 'Have the blasted money, Dido.' He shoves it into my bag. I expect him to insist on getting on with me, but he stays on the pavement. 'I wish you well, Dido!' he cries. 'I wish you a long and happy life!' The bus pulls away. Feeling really bad again, I wave goodbye.

But then the relief of being back among those cheerful yellow poles and seeing the word ALDGATE sliding along the black strips. I'd been out to the very edge of things, but now I'm travelling back, the enormous orange sun setting behind me. Packs of schoolkids get on, laughing, squabbling, shrieking, munching crisps. And then they're gone, and there's just the roar of the train, and it's dark, and the train is reflected in its own windows. The two women sitting next to me are going to do their Christmas shopping. One of them is going to buy Iconic Drops for Misty, and an Amazon Echo for Ben. I think of the £200 in my bag, and whether I should tag along with them to Oxford Street, go on a spending spree, or whether to stuff it into the man at Aldgate's cup and tell him he should take the tinsel off his poor dog. The track straightens, and I can see far along the train, all the way to where a white girl in gold baggy trousers is filming a black girl in a pink tutu doing gymnastics around a yellow pole. I think of the ballerina in the photograph and her little monster, and it clutches my heart. Then the tutu girl goes into a backbend, hands gripping the pole, climbing downwards to the speckled floor. And I love the way London is so itself, so London-ish, and how everyone in it – lovers, loners, natives, settlers, fugitives, visitors, underdogs, fat cats – we are all part of its dance.

And at Finchley Road; the orange puffer jacket, the mop of black hair, and the book sticking out of his pocket. When he sees me, he cries, 'Ha!' and looks around, lifting his hands in a question. I laugh, and shrug, and lift my hands too.

'You got rid of him in the end!' He shouts it over the beeping of the closing doors.

'Yes, I did.' I think of the pigeon's eyes, glassy orange buttons, and then of Paul Fildes' eyes, that violet intensity. 'It's for the best,' said the reading man. 'It was never going to work out between you two.' And then, even though there are a few spare seats, he glances at my bag and my heart lifts, and I lift my bag, and he sits down.

The Invisible

Jo Lloyd

Across the lake

Mr Ingram and his Invisible daughter Miss Ingram live close by, Martha tells us, in a grand, impractical mansion of the type the wealthy favour – except Invisible, of course – made from dressed stone the colour of spring cream, with a slate roof and glass in every window.

Is that so, we say.

They receive numerous Invisible guests, Martha tells us, who must travel here from other Invisible mansions, in other parts of the country.

That would follow, we say.

They attend fairs and sales about the district. They are regulars at our Wednesday markets.

To sell or to buy?

They are Invisible!

To accomplish trade, both parties must be visible, a fact we have not previously had cause to contemplate.

Mr Ingram's mansion, Martha tells us, stands on the other side of the lake, at the foot of the mountain. We have inspected the spot she indicates and confirmed it is in no way remarkable. Cold eels of water slide among rushes and sedges and tumps of starry moss. Cat-gorse and furze cling to rafts of drier ground. Spearwort and flag dip their toes and shiver.

Not that we need to search for evidence. If there were a mansion across the lake, our dogs would be howling every time an Ingram passed by. Our daughters would be scouring their pots, our sons sweating in their stables and gardens.

Some accuse Martha of fraud, although what she has to gain by it we cannot determine.

Others say her wits are failing. We've known her put her clothes on back to front and summon her cow with the call meant for hogs. She will stop for minutes on end to watch rooks or lapwings tumble about the sky, as if they bore porridge and dates and the answers to life's mysteries in their beaks.

But most are happy, eager even, to take her at her word. We want to believe that the Invisible have, for whatever purpose, established their Invisible home next to us. It pleases us to imagine them prodding the fat rumps of our livestock, testing our grains with their clean, Invisible fingernails.

Tell us more, we say, and Martha dimples like a girl.

There are many of them, she says. Sometimes the Invisible outnumber other visitors.

But why do they come to market?

For amusement, I suppose. Entertainment.

We look each other up and down, wondering which of us is most entertaining.

The Ingrams have called at Martha's cottage, of an evening, to pay their respects.

Miss Ingram has such pale hands, Martha says. As if she keeps them folded away in a linen chest.

What language do they speak?

It is English, I presume. I seem to understand some of it. But their speech is strange. Until you are very close, it's like a noise of leaves or water.

We cannot think why, of all of us, they would choose Martha. She is not the most educated or wise. Not even the most gullible.

Invite us along next time they visit, says Jacob. That should sort the wheat from the goats.

They wouldn't allow it, Martha says.

What are you afraid of? Jacob says. Let's settle this once and for all.

Come on Martha, we say. Let's settle this. Unless you have reason to be afraid.

I would love to see Miss Ingram's dress, says Eliza. And her jewellery. I would love to see how she does her hair.

Oh yes, we say. We'd love to see her dress and her hair and her jewellery.

It's out of the question, Martha keeps saying. They would never agree.

But if there is one thing we know, it is persistence.

Freckled peas

The Vestry can find no regulations that apply. In the past, Martha might have been suspected of contracting with demons, but the Parliament in London has repealed the law against witchcraft. We don't know if this is because we've progressed beyond such superstition or because all the witches have been drowned.

Martha has never been known as a fool or a liar. Once she claimed to have seen a yellow cat the size of a two-tooth hogget at her door, but perhaps she did, and if not, anyone could make that mistake. Jacob complained that she sold him a calf that was already sick and it expired within a day, but they resolved that dispute between them. Mostly she has lived the way we all do, evenly, tidily, respecting time and season. She plants oats and beans and freckled peas on her late father's holding, keeps bees and chickens, drives her cow to the grazings. She has no husband or children bringing home a wage from the quarry, but then she has no one for whom she must buy tea and sugar. She is a hard worker, if a slow one. When she was a baby her mother, Rebecca, stumbling, as we understand, let her fall in the hearth. In the moments it took the parents to react, flames bit through the swaddling, gnawed the tender infant limbs. We found Rebecca later in the church porch, hanged dead. Martha was left with a limp and, in her breath, a hiss as of hot ashes settling. But she is not one to make excuses. She salts her own bacon, gathers her own turf and bark. She has a reputation as a pickler and preserver, putting up the greater part of her harvest and whatever she collects from woods and wastes. She's able to sell her surplus to lazier households. She is careful with her animals, keeping them clean and dry. In hard winters, she stints herself to feed them.

Plump and handsome

Martha is adamant that the Invisible are not the Tylwyth Teg, who are known to be short and ill-favoured.

The Ingrams are as tall as we are, she points out. Taller. They're plump and handsome.

Also the Tylwyth Teg are spiteful. They bear grudges for generations. They hide robins' eggs in shoes, crumble owl pellets into the flour.

The Invisible, Martha says, are smiling always, and if they are not smiling, they are laughing. They are generous. Once I saw Miss Ingram pick up a fallen kit and place it back with its fellows.

But on further questioning, she admits such acts of charity are rare. Mostly the Invisible keep apart, chattering among themselves.

How do they dress?

It is the fashion of the city, I suppose, all bright colours and embroidery. And everything always new. Not darned or frayed or even muddy. As if every day is Easter Day.

Do any of them resemble your father? John Protheroe the smith wants to know. Or Price Price or Mother Jenkins?

But we hush him. We don't want to think that the contents of our graveyard have got themselves up in their best clothes to trot about among us, formulating opinions.

Martha shakes her head. They're not like anyone I've seen before. In looks or behaviour. I believe they're different from us altogether.

Only child

Martha's limp identifies her from some distance. It is of the lurching, stiff-legged variety, like a boat hit side-on by a swell. She uses a stick, for walking only, never hitting. When a beast jibs or straggles, she chides, like a doting granny, in a voice you could mistake for praise. She combs the burs from her cow's tail. Sometimes, milking, she seems to fall asleep with her head on Pluen's flank.

The only child of only children, since Enoch her father died, Martha has no family at all. She can breakfast at midnight if she pleases, not even trouble to prepare dinner. She has grown thinner these last years. If there were a tempest, such as our forebears talked of, strong enough to strip the thatch from our roofs and topple animals in their stalls, it might blow Martha away altogether, leaving only her shawl hooked in a blackthorn.

Enoch wanted Martha to marry Abel Pritchard. There was a conversation and a handshake and for months Pritchard would call to smoke a pipe or play chess with Enoch. On Sundays, Pritchard would walk her to church, and a comical pairing they made, Martha bobbing in the lee of his ox plod. But in the end he found a girl younger and quicker, with a dowry worth the promise. The bitterness between Enoch and Pritchard lasted until the older man's death. We do not know what Martha thought.

The Reverends

The Reverend Doctor Clough-Vaughan-Bowen comes all the way from the next county to see

Martha. He lodges with the Reverend Rice-Mansel-Evans and, early next morning, the two men pick their way through a sparkling drizzle to the door of her cottage. Doctor Clough-Vaughan-Bowen is a learned man, of good family. He has written scholarly works, we understand, on subjects of interest to the clergy – adult baptism or the wearing of the chasuble. Rumour says he had a wife who died giving birth to their dying child. Rumour shrugs. When our neighbours and families suffer such losses we take gifts of hyssop or honey to their door, weep with them beside the new graves. But it is hard to believe that men such as Doctor Clough-Vaughan-Bowen have feelings as sharp or deep as our own. Mwynig and Brithen, we remember, bellow through the night that their calves are taken, but next day turn their inquiries instead to turnips.

The Reverend Doctor has not come to reprimand Martha, nor to interrogate her. He talks, in his educated, university English, of which she comprehends a third at most, of many invisible things. Hopes and dreams and memories. The brains of horses. The souls of the dead. The imagination. The future. The swallows sleeping snugly at the bottom of the lake.

He talks of the visible, and the traces it leaves. The fountain that sprang up where the saint pressed his thumb into the earth. The rock pierced by the giant's spear. The stony pawprint left by Arthur's hound hunting Twrch Trwyth across the mountain tops.

You see what I'm saying? he says to Martha.

Martha smiles and nods at moments where it seems appropriate.

The drizzle gives way to stumps of rainbow parting a watery sky. The reverends pick their way back and Doctor Clough-Vaughan-Bowen takes his leave, apparently satisfied.

French sauce

Martha has pressed her nose to the windows of Mr Ingram's mansion. The Invisible dine late, she tells us, but they light neither candle nor lamp. There is no fire even, but they seem warm enough in their cambrics and silks. The ladies' throats and wrists are bare. They drink wine as red as rosehips from silver goblets. The china is blue and white, thin as a blade, and the table is laid with many dishes. They eat roast meats with French sauce, fillets and cheeks and sirloins, veal fricassey, veal ragoo, snipe, partridge, wheatears, lark livers simmered with cloves, blanched lettuce, white milk-bread, parsley and sweet herbs chopped fine, flummery and posset, clary fritters, heaped bowls of gooseberries and mulberries and quinces, sweetmeats coloured with spinach and beet and delicately fashioned into multitudinous shapes.

But who waits at table? we want to know. Who delivers the food? Who cooks it?

Martha has seen no Invisible footmen standing to attention, no butchers or vintners at the kitchen door. The Invisible, she insists, are all wealthy. There are no Invisible maids or carpenters or shopkeepers. The Invisible do no work.

But how can they live without the poor to serve them? we ask.

What about the puddings, says Eliza. Are they spiced? Do they wobble? Are they eaten hot or cold?

There are baked puddings and boiled puddings and set puddings, says Martha. Wonderful domed and turreted puddings, like palaces. Thick with candied cherries and angelica. The custard is yellow as buttercups.

They sit at table for hours, she tells us, but they talk more than they chew. They don't gobble their food or help it to their mouths with their fingers, hunting down any fragments that fall and cramming them back in.

Tell us about the meats, we say. Tell us about the cream. Tell us about the apricots and persimmons, the roast swans and haunches of venison. Tell us.

Englyn

We are enjoying a kind of fame. In other districts the gossip is of Martha. The Ingrams are mentioned in a number of sermons. The Dissenters make it yet another opportunity to talk of ale and tithes. Owen Owen composes an englyn on the subject of the Invisible that is perhaps not up to the standard of his early and most beautiful work, but we admire its wisdom and one particularly melodious alliteration, and some of us learn it to recite to our families as we sit beside our hearths.

Markets are visibly better attended and at first we are grateful. But many of the newcomers spend only time, which they use to query and argue, cast aspersions, search behind walls and under trestles, inside calf cots and pig sties.

If anyone asks what makes us so interesting, we have no answer. We cannot explain the Invisible's curiosity. Some of us speculate it may be convenience, a matter of location. Some of us wonder if the attention is always kindly meant. Do they wrinkle their noses as they walk past us? Wave their lace handkerchiefs to clear the air? Do they avert their eyes from our misshapen bodies and pocked faces?

Mr Ingram has a gold pocketwatch. He consults it more often than is strictly necessary for someone who has no appointments to keep.

Ribbon

Some of the young people – Naomi Price and Megan Prosser and their tittering friends, plus one or two lads who are sweet on them, and Mot, the Prices' brindled cattle dog – have taken to aping the behaviour of the Invisible. They practise walking in no special direction and raising their eyebrows while others labour. They affect amazement at sickles and stooks and handlooms and potherbs and piglets. The girls have acquired a silk ribbon that they pass about between them so that one or another, usually Naomi, can wear it in her hair every day. They hold their skirts out of the mud, in the manner of Miss Ingram, and fan themselves with sprays of hawthorn.

They have developed a sudden passion for knowledge, pestering Martha with questions. She indulges them until she tires or runs out of observations and then she shoes them away like so many finches. The next day they flock back, nudging and giggling, as at their first day of dame school. Martha tuts fondly and repeats yesterday's lesson.

We think it harmless enough until they neglect their work. Three times, John Protheroe has to fetch his boy back to the forge. There is a great deal of shouting and a coulter is spoiled.

Megan judges herself too good to dip rushes, while Naomi protests that stitching or churning will roughen her hands. The Prices are accustomed to their daughter's airs, but she has corrupted the once-faithful Mot, who now slinks away from his duties at every opportunity to bury his head in Naomi's knees and sigh as she folds his pretty ears into a bow.

The Ingrams should know better than to encourage such foolishness, we say to Martha. You should know better.

And when some of us point out that young folk rarely need encouragement, no one listens.

We must keep them close to home, we say.

The dog can be tied up, but our children need another solution. We give them more chores, more responsibilities, make sure they are too tired for mischief.

For a time, we think things back to normal. But the Protheroe boy wears a look of discontent as he works the bellows, and young Preece leans daydreaming on a shovel, next to the lime he should be spreading. As for Naomi, she has declared she will never marry. She would rather stay a spinster, she says, than grow red-cheeked and loose-waisted with a man whose favourite subject is the pigs he smells of. She can be seen rehearsing for her preferred future, strolling alone through marble halls or colonnades of pleached limes, her nose in the air and a frayed gold ribbon trailing behind.

Unnavigable

It is July and there has been no rain for five weeks. The summer pastures have scorched yellow, then black, as if they have combusted from within, and we bring the herds down early. The lake shrinks. Insects clump and die in its rotting margins. Springs that have never before failed run dry. When the cows complain of their multiple empty stomachs, we offer them leaves and twigs. Harvests are poor all about the district.

The Invisible are enjoying the sun, Martha tells us. They walk out at full midday to admire unclimbable heights and horrible precipices. Their hats are large. They spread cloths on the ground before they sit. They picnic on assorted meats, potted and pastried and aspiced. They do a kind of dancing, the figures intricate and indecipherable.

What is the music? we want to know. Who plays?

Martha shakes her head. There are no musicians. It is in the air perhaps. They take it with them.

Rain falls every day of September. The drops gather and hang in fleecy clouds until the commons resemble the floor of a shearing shed. The earth, muddled by these disorderly seasons, squanders her energies on green shoots that will not last the winter.

It turns hot again. Haf bach Mihangel. The sunsets are bronze, the dawns like unripe strawberries. The new quarry drops its prices. There is an accident in which two men die and one loses the use of his arm.

The Invisible are busy at their sports and pastimes. Not throwing or sparring or chasing a leather ball. Games with mysterious rules and objectives. Mr Ingram covers his eyes and the others circle around him, calling and pointing. Miss Ingram gestures like a bird, or an old woman, and they all laugh. They tilt and balance and yaw and hop and fall. There is no winner. Or they are all winners. It is hard to tell.

November. The storms beat at our walls, howling accusations. When the winds drop, the bone chill starts. We count the jars, measure what's left in barrels and sacks. Every creak is a stranger creeping through the darkness with intent. December. We muffle our noses, warm our hands in our armpits. At night we hug our husbands and children close to steal their heat. The salted meat is used, the pickles and dried fruit gone. We boil hide to make broth. January. February. Those with a cow are drinking milk and praying the hay will last. Those without are living on husks and air. The Prossers have sold their bedding and only a blanket donated by the Reverend keeps their youngest from perishing.

The Ingrams must look across the lake, see our cottages dimly lit, some without smoke even. Do they imagine us huddled inside, stupid with cold, our fingers white?

In the second half of March, there is a run of dewy bright mornings. The milfyw flowers, and we put the cattle out to graze. They skip and buck like the ogre's darling children, dip their heads to the celandines to admire their bristled chins. A soft breeze strokes our hair and we hold our faces to the sun. The frogs croak all night. The sparrows get busy in our roofs and we in our beds.

But one afternoon the sky is spotted with peewits and golden plovers, fieldfares and redwings. They wheel above us, calling their alarm, then the snow they are fleeing arrives. It is the heaviest fall in ten years, heaping against walls, holding our doors closed. By morning, earth and air are so white that half a mile from us a new shore seems to have formed, before a strange, unnavigable sea. It is days before we can drive our animals to pasture, and when we do, bird corpses litter the

ground, too many even for the foxes, and the grass
is stewed.

When Martha limps into view we forget to
ask how she is managing and instead inquire after
the Invisible. How do they like the winter? Do
they startle when the wind jeers from their
chimneys? Do their slates seal out the thaw?

They play cards. They enjoy jugged hare and
buttered peas, sugar cakes enrobed in sugar. Miss
Ingram's frock is lilac, lit from within like a
spring sky.

We look at each other. We frown.

Some propose going to the Ingrams' door to
beg for work or, failing that, last night's bones or
a measure of barley. We should get up a committee,
perhaps, to remind the Ingrams of their duty to
their neighbours. Some even mutter of going in
force. We will don dresses and bonnets for
disguise, paint our faces white, light torches.

But some object. We don't need violence.
Martha will help us. Let us be there when they visit,
we say, as we have said before. Let us talk to them.

Tell me your demands, she says. I will represent
you.

But it is not enough. We want to make our
own case. We want to hear how they respond.
Many of us are wiser than Martha. Many of us
know more English. We will not be denied.

The Ingrams abhor questions, she says, or importuning.

We will be quiet. We will only speak when spoken to.

They cannot bear any light but that of the sun and the moon.

We are accustomed to darkness, we say.

Creaks and ventings

In the twilight borrowed from a clear night sky, we recognise our neighbours' heads and shoulders, their creaks and ventings, familiar from vigils and services. That is Widow Johns, that is Eliza, that is young Jenkin Jenkins, taking advantage of the situation to slide up close to Mary Probert. That is mice hurrying in the thatch. That is Pluen at the other end of the room, grumbling about a greasy trough or spiders in her hay. We yawn and sigh and stretch and fidget. We listen.

And finally we hear something. We think we hear something. A padding that is the approach of feet softer than a cat's, feet that make no mark on the ground. A noise as of leaves or water, gradually increasing.

Then a figure rises before us. A figure that is quite obviously, even in this dusk, Jacob, with a shawl draped over his head. He starts speaking, or piping rather, in a high-pitched voice, words that are not words in any language we know. We aren't sure what to do. Beneath his trill, an undercurrent of confusion and dismay begins.

Come along now, that's enough of that, says Old Mr Jenkins.

Jacob keeps on babbling and chirping. He totters in a circle, flaps a lunatic hand. Almost falls over Martha stepping forward to protest, almost saves himself, staggers again, knocks her to the floor.

Then we are all up, talking at once, cheering and booing and baying, like a crowd at a hanging. Some help Martha, others pull the cover from Jacob's head. He is laughing. In a minute a rushlight is burning. Our faces glow red and orange, outraged, amused, disgusted, disappointed.

So much for your Invisible, says Jacob, cackling. And some of us cackle with him. So much for lies and nonsense. So much for anyone who thinks themselves better than us.

Martha has her face in her hands and Eliza is comforting her, turning every now and then to berate Jacob. Look what you've done, says Eliza. And some of us join in. Look what you've done. They will never come now.

Pullet

We scold Jacob until he agrees to apologise. He presents himself at Martha's cottage with a speckled pullet under his arm. She shuts the door in their faces.

Although, in the matter of Jacob's behaviour, our sympathies lie with Martha, the incident is not unwelcome to everyone. His method was crude, we admit, but he has expressed our own misgivings.

Others are confident that Jacob's stunt has only delayed our meeting with the Invisible. Next time, we say, we will be more particular with our invitations.

Martha herself seems to have aged years overnight, as elderly people sometimes do, in a sudden haste to know their end. She will not discuss the abortive visit, nor will she deliver fresh news. Tell us what the Ingrams are up to, we say. Have there been parties or excursions? A masked ball perhaps? But she will say nothing.

For a time, we make do with other topics. White peas reach double the price of wheat. Sucking pigs are 15s a head. John Johns and Ruth Prosser break their engagement and, a month later, mend it. Rachel Protheroe gives birth to twins. The hay is affected by mildew. In the next parish, we hear, a cow is struck by lightning and her calf bleaches white, not a shred of colour left in it. That, we think, is something Miss Ingram might wish to see. But when we say this to Martha, she turns her back.

Some point to Martha's silence as evidence of deceit. Others defend her.

It is shameful, we say, to treat an old woman with so little respect.

There must be respect on both sides, we respond.

We'd sooner listen to Martha than to mischief-makers, we say.

Fools are the best audience for foolery, we reply.

Rancour and rebuke creep among us like fleas. Friends fall out. Families almost come to blows. Some of us declare ourselves fed up with the whole business and ready to agree with anyone who will leave us in peace.

We start gathering fuel for next winter. We will stack it high this year, make a wall we cannot see over. As harvest arrives, we watch our neighbours at their crops and do not offer to help. When it is our turn, they reciprocate.

Martha has become increasingly solitary. She is gaining a reputation for rudeness. She tells the Reverend's wife to keep her baked goods to herself. She shouts at two of the smallest Prossers until they run home crying. She rarely comes to market. When we do see her, we observe that her limp is more pronounced. She stops to rest often.

Eliza brings us reports. Martha has a cough that will not mend. She is several times confined to her bed. We bring her the treats invalids are thought to enjoy, borage tea and calves' feet. She has no appetite. We keep her fire burning, milk Pluen, feed the chickens. I'm not dying, am I? she asks, waking from troubled sleep. When she does, we will only need tell the bees.

Shadow

There is a new prime minister in London. Laws are repealed, laws are passed. Perhaps moths will benefit from the candle tax and robbers from improvements in the highways. Nobody asks our opinion. Like grass, we are meant to thrive unattended, underfoot.

We watch the road and the bridge. We look especially hard at visitors on market days. In early winter, when a light snow falls, we walk around the lake. We see prints of fox, polecat, badger. Nothing else. As we turn for home, the powder squeaks, curling our spines.

If we were rich as the Ingrams, we say, we would put up a stone drinking fountain and have our name carved on it for all to read. We would build clocktowers and almshouses and schools. They would all bear our name.

Winter closes around us again. We have no heart for the seasonal festivities. We leave the wren in the hedge, the mistletoe in the trees, the mare's skull in the barn. We burn through our ramparts of fuel.

To no one's astonishment, the Prossers lose their cow. Fecklessness, we whisper. We should take them some of our own milk, a little oatmeal too. Perhaps tomorrow, we say, moving our feet closer to the fire.

When spring comes we are still alive. The day comes up a glistening mist briefly suffused with mallow. We dig and trench, plant peas and early cabbages, blister our hands and break our backs. We inspect the walls and ditches we repaired this time last year, this time the year before. Some of us patch a gap here or there, some of us shrug and stare into the distance. The sun falls through the haze like a scarlet millstone.

The Protheroe boy and Naomi Price run off in the night, gone to Liverpool, we learn, to seek their fortune in the Americas. John Preece gets an apprenticeship in Bristol. He will be his own master one day, he boasts, master of others. He will be an alderman, a mayor, with glass windows in his house and a gold chain around his neck.

We give the pigs extra barley, thinking this year we will feed them until they are too fat to walk. They will have to sit down, like little gentlemen, to take their last meal. We will kill them early, have a feast whose memory will warm us through the cold months. Chops and ribs and belly and brisket, liver and lights and blood pudding. We will eat from one breakfast to the next, saving nothing. If we need a rest, we will lay our heads right there on the table.

Sometimes, as we go about our day, a shadow falls. A blackbird clatters in unprovoked alarm. Sometimes we think we see figures on the stone bridge. They have no occupation other than leaning and an ease, leaning, that none of our visible neighbours could achieve. They are looking in our direction. We almost think they are looking at us. We lower our eyes and walk the other way.

But at night we cannot sleep for thinking of them, across the lake, drifting on pallets of down and feather. And we wonder if they ever dream of us, or only of morning, when they will come stepping through the rushes, pocketwatches in their pale hands, passing through us like a breeze through leaves, a wave through water.

Notes

Tylwyth Teg – not fair and not people.

Twrch Trwyth – the cursed but well-coiffed prince boar.

Englyn – a short and obedient verse.

Haf bach Mihangel – the little summer that we enjoy about Michaelmastime, when we must pay our rents.

Milfyw – the plant called by Linnaeus *Luzula campestris;* when it appears, we read poetry to the cows.

About the Authors

Lucy Caldwell was born in Belfast in 1981. She is the author of three novels, several stage plays and radio dramas, two collections of short stories (*Multitudes*, 2016, and *Intimacies*, forthcoming in May 2020), and is the editor of the anthology *Being Various: New Irish Short Stories* (Faber, 2019). Awards include the Rooney Prize for Irish Literature, the George Devine Award, the Dylan Thomas Prize, the Imison Award, the Susan Smith Blackburn Award, the Irish Writers' and Screenwriters' Guild Award, the Commonwealth Writers' Award (Canada & Europe), the Edge Hill University Short Story Prize Readers' Choice Award, a Fiction Uncovered Award, a K. Blundell Trust Award and a Major Individual Artist Award from the Arts Council of Northern Ireland. Lucy was elected a Fellow of the Royal Society of Literature in 2018. She was previously shortlisted for the BBC International Short Story Award in 2012.

Lynda Clark is a former bookseller and videogame producer. Her short story, 'Ghillie's Mum', won the 2018 Commonwealth Writers' Award (Canada & Europe), received a special mention in Galley Beggars Press Short Story Prize 2016/17, and was published by *Granta* online. Another story, 'Grandma's Feast Day', was shortlisted for The Cambridge Short Story Prize 2017 and is forthcoming in a collection from TSS Publishing. Lynda's debut novel, *Beyond Kidding*, will be published by Fairlight Books in October 2019. Lynda also has a PhD in interactive narrative and is currently a Research and Development Fellow in Narrative and Play at the University of Dundee.

Jacqueline Crooks is a Jamaican-born writer. Her short stories have been published by *MsLexia*, *Granta* and Virago, and she was featured in the Breaking Ground list of the Best British Writers of Colour. Her collection, *The Ice Migration* (Peepal Tree Press, 2018), was longlisted for the 2019 Orwell Prize in the Political Fiction category, and she has also been shortlisted for the Ashram and Wasafiri New Writing awards. Jacqueline has a degree in Social Policy from Roehampton University of Surrey and an MA in Creative and Life Writing from Goldsmiths University. She delivers writing workshops to socially excluded communities, primarily older people, refugees and asylum seekers, disadvantaged children and young people.

Tamsin Grey grew up in England, Scotland and Zambia. She has worked as a cucumber picker, a yoga teacher, an oral historian, and as a speechwriter to a secretary of state. Her first novel, *She's Not There*, was published by The Borough Press in 2018 to critical acclaim. Tamsin works part-time as a civil servant, and is currently interviewing colleagues across Whitehall about their experiences of working on EU Exit. She is also writing her second novel, set at a music festival.

Jo Lloyd's short stories have appeared in *The Best British Short Stories 2012* (Salt), *Zoetrope: All-Story, Ploughshares, Southern Review,* and elsewhere. Her short story, 'The Earth, Thy Great Exchequer, Ready Lies' featured in The O. Henry Prize Stories 2018, widely regarded as the most prestigious awards for short fiction in the US. Jo has also previously won an Asham Award, the Willesden Herald International Short Story Prize, and a McGinnis-Ritchie Award. She grew up in South Wales and has recently returned to live there.

About the BBC National Short Story Award with Cambridge University

The BBC National Short Story Award is one of the most prestigious for a single short story and celebrates the best in home-grown short fiction. The ambition of the award, which is now in its fourteenth year, is to expand opportunities for British writers, readers and publishers of the short story, and honour the UK's finest exponents of the form. The award is a highly regarded feature within the literary landscape with a justified reputation for genuinely changing writers' careers.

James Lasdun secured the inaugural award in 2006 for 'An Anxious Man'. In 2012, when the Award expanded internationally for one year to mark the London Olympics, the Bulgarian writer Miroslav Penkov was victorious with his story 'East of the West'. Last year's winner, 'The Sweet Sop' by Ingrid Persaud, was 'tender and ebullient, heartbreaking and full of humour', with a unique voice and emotional power, relaying the story of a young Trinidadian man reunited with his absent father via the power of chocolate. Previous alumni include Lionel Shriver, Zadie Smith, Hilary Mantel, Jon McGregor, Rose Tremain, Sarah Hall and William Trevor.

The winning author receives £15,000, and four further shortlisted authors £600 each. All five shortlisted stories are broadcast on BBC Radio 4 along with interviews with the writers.

In 2015, to mark the National Short Story Award's tenth anniversary, the BBC Young Writers' Award was launched in order to inspire the next generation of short story writers, to raise the profile of the form with a younger audience, and provide an outlet for their creative labours. The teenage writers shortlisted for the award have their stories recorded and broadcast on BBC Radio 1 and featured online, and have a writing workshop with one of the writer judges. The winner of the 2018 award was 17-year-old Davina Bacon from Cambridgeshire for 'Under a Deep Blue Sky', a raw and emotionally powerful short story about a young African poacher and the brutal murder of a mother and baby elephant. It was inspired by her early years living in Africa and her passion for the environment. Previous winners include Brennig Davies for 'Skinning', Lizzie Freestone for 'Ode to a Boy Musician', and Elizabeth Ryder for 'The Roses'.

To inspire the next generation of short story readers, teenagers around the UK are also involved in the BBC National Short Story Award via the BBC Student Critics' Award, which gives selected 16–18 year olds the opportunity to read, listen to, discuss and critique the five stories shortlisted by the judges, and have their say. The students are supported with discussion guides, teaching resources and interactions with writers and judges, for an enriching experience that brings literature to life.

The year 2018 marked the start of an exciting collaboration between the BBC and the University of Cambridge and First Story. The University of Cambridge supports all three awards, and hosts an annual short story festival at the Institute of Continuing Education, which offers a range of creative writing and English Literature programmes, and curates an exclusive online exhibition of artefacts drawn from the University Library's archive to inspire and intrigue entrants of the Young Writers' Award. The charity First Story bring their experience in fostering creativity, confidence and writing skills in secondary schools serving low-income communities to bear, by supporting the Young

Writers' Award and the Student Critics' Award with activity engaging young people with reading, writing and listening to short stories.

The 2019 BBC National Short Story Award with Cambridge University was chaired by Nikki Bedi, a television and radio broadcaster with a passion for making arts and culture accessible. Nikki currently curates, writes and presents The Arts Hour on the BBC World Service, their flagship arts and culture programme, which once a month becomes The Arts Hour On Tour, a show that travels across the globe to different countries bringing the hottest names, talents and issues to the airwaves and to 79 million listeners. Her recent television work includes 'The Road To Englistan', a special BBC 2 in-depth interview with actor Riz Ahmed in New York, and BBC2's topical, weekly arts and entertainment programme Front Row. Nikki is a regular interviewer and presenter on BBC Radio 4's Loose Ends and has presented Front Row and Woman's Hour on the same station. Nikki also hosts the Virgin Media Business podcast Voom and has had some of the world's greatest entrepreneurs and disruptors chatting to her in the studio. Born to an Indian father and English mother, Nikki began her career in Mumbai as both a stage and film actress and worked with some of India's finest directors.

Her foray into the world of presenting came when the UK's Channel 4 gave her a talk show, Bombay Chat, and its success prompted Star TV in Asia to give her a primetime chat show called Nikki Tonight which became Asia's most widely viewed and also most controversial talk show.

After spending time living and working in Los Angeles, Nikki returned to the UK to become the face of Universal's film channel The Studio and also presented the live movie show Worldwide Screen on NOW TV.

Bedi is joined by an esteemed group of award-winning writers on the panel. Richard Beard's six novels include *Lazarus is Dead, Dry Bones* and *Damascus*, which was a *New York Times* Notable Book of the Year. His most recent novel, *Acts of the Assassins,* was shortlisted for the Goldsmiths Prize 2015, and he is the author of four books of narrative non-fiction, including his memoir *The Day That Went Missing* which won the 2018 PEN Ackerley Award for literary autobiography.

Daisy Johnson's first novel, *Everything Under*, was shortlisted for the 2018 Man Booker Prize, making her the youngest author ever to be on the shortlist. Her debut book, the short story collection *Fen*, won the 2017 Edge Hill Short Story Prize. She currently lives in Oxford by the river.

Cynan Jones was born near Aberaeron on the west coast of Wales in 1975. He is the author of five novels, published in over 20 countries. He has been longlisted and shortlisted for numerous prizes internationally, and won the Wales Book of the Year Fiction Prize, a Betty Trask Award, the Jerwood Fiction Uncovered Award, and the 2017 BBC National Short Story Award. He has also written stories for BBC Radio, a screenplay for the hit crime drama *Hinterland*, and a collection of tales for children. Other writing has appeared in numerous anthologies and newspapers, and in journals and magazines including *Granta* and *The New Yorker*.

Di Speirs is the Books Editor, BBC Radio. She edited the Woman's Hour serial for three years, produced the first ever Book of the Week, and has directed many Book at Bedtimes as well as dramas. She now leads the London Readings team and is the Editor for Open Book and Book Club on BBC Radio 4 and World Book Club on the BBC World Service. A long-time advocate of the formidable power of the short story, she has been closely involved in the BBC National Short Story Award since its inception thirteen years ago and is the regular judge on the panel.

For more information on the awards, please visit www.bbc.co.uk/nssa and www.bbc.co.uk/ywa. You can also keep up-to-date on Twitter via #BBCNSSA, #BBCYWA and #shortstories.

Award Partners

BBC Radio 4 is the world's biggest single commissioner of short stories, which attract more than a million listeners. Contemporary stories are broadcast every week, the majority of which are specially commissioned throughout the year. www.bbc.co.uk/radio4

BBC Radio 1 is the UK's No.1 youth station, targeting 15 to 29 year-olds with a distinctive mix of new music and programmes focusing on issues affecting young people. One of the station's key purposes is to support new British music and emerging artists, also discovering new artists through BBC Introducing. Radio 1 is also the leading voice for young people in the UK, tackling relevant issues through our documentaries, Radio 1's Life Hacks, Newsbeat as well as our social action and education campaigns. Topics covered include youth employment, sexuality, body image and bullying. BBC Radio 1 is a truly multiplatform station, enabling young audiences to connect to the network and to listen, watch and share great content both at home and whilst on the move – via FM and DAB Radio; the BBC iPlayer Radio app; online, Freeview and other digital television platforms; and via mobile. www.bbc.co.uk/radio1

First Story believes there is dignity and power in being able to tell your own story, and that writing can transform lives. We're working towards a society that encourages and supports all young people to write creatively for pleasure and agency. We're committed to bringing opportunities for creativity to students who may not otherwise have the chance. Our flagship programme places professional writers into secondary schools serving low-income communities, where they work intensively with students and teachers to foster confidence, creativity and writing ability. Through our core programme and extended activities, we expand young people's horizons and raise aspirations. Participants gain vital skills that underpin academic attainment and support achieving potential. Find out more and get involved at firststory.org.uk

The mission of the **University of Cambridge** is to contribute to society through the pursuit of education, learning and research at the highest international levels of excellence. To date, 107 affiliates of the University have won the Nobel Prize. Founded in 1209, the University comprises 31 autonomous Colleges, which admit undergraduates and provide small-group tuition, and 150 departments, faculties and institutions. The University sits at the heart of one of the world's largest technology clusters. The 'Cambridge Phenomenon' has created 1,500 hi-tech companies, 14 of them valued at over US$1 billion and two at over US$10 billion. Cambridge promotes the interface between academia and business, and has a global reputation for innovation. The BBC National Short Story Award is being supported by the School of Arts and Humanities, Faculty of English, University Library and the new University of Cambridge Centre for Creative Writing which is part of the University of Cambridge Institute of Continuing Education, which provides courses to members of the public. www.cam.ac.uk

Previous Winners

2018: 'The Sweet Sop' by Ingrid Persaud

2017: 'The Edge of the Shoal' by Cynan Jones

2016: 'Disappearances' by KJ Orr
Runner-up: 'Morning, Noon & Night'
by Claire-Louise Bennett

2015: 'Briar' by Jonathan Buckley
Runner-up: 'Bunny' by Mark Haddon

2014: 'Kilifi Creek' by Lionel Shriver
Runner-up: 'Miss Adele Amidst the Corsets'
by Zadie Smith

2013: 'Mrs Fox' by Sarah Hall
Runner-up: 'Notes from the House Spirits'
by Lucy Wood

2012: 'East of the West' by Miroslav Penkov
Runner-up: 'Sanctuary by Henrietta Rose-Innes

2011: 'The Dead Roads' by D W Wilson
Runner-up: 'Wires' by Jon McGregor

2010: 'Tea at the Midland' by David Constantine
Runner-up: 'If It Keeps On Raining'
by Jon McGregor

2009: 'The Not-Dead & the Saved' by Kate Clanchy
Runner-up: 'Moss Witch' by Sara Maitland

2008: 'The Numbers' by Clare Wigfall
Runner-up: 'The People on Privilege Hill'
by Jane Gardam

2007: 'The Orphan and the Mob' by Julian Gough
Runner-up: 'Slog's Dad' by David Almond

2006: 'An Anxious Man' by James Lasdun
Runner-up: 'The Safehouse' by Michel Faber